THE DEVIL'S HORSEWHIP

DEVIL'S HORSEWHIP
THE

A Barbican First by

DAMION SPENCER

Published by Barbican Press
London, Los Angeles

Registered UK office: 1 Ashenden Road, London E5 0DP
US office: 852 21st Street, Unit E, Santa Monica CA 90403

www.barbicanpress.com
@barbicanpress1

A CIP catalogue for this book is available from the British Library

Distributed in North America by Publishers Group West

Cover art by Pablo Gerardo Camacho
Author photograph by Tia Haygood courtesy of TopTia Photography

ISBN: 978-1-917352-02-4
eISBN: 978-1-917352-03-1

'Bunka Bat and Sour Orange' was first published in Volume 35 of *The Caribbean Writer Journal*.

An earlier version of 'Bull Buck and Duppy Conqueror' was published in Volume 37 of *The Caribbean Writer Journal*.

'Death Comes in Threes' was first published on the *Wasafiri* website.

'A Handful of Bush Violets' (excerpt from 'The Devil's Horsewhip') will be published in Volume 39 of *The Caribbean Writer Journal*.

 **Damion Spencer** is originally from St. Mary in Jamaica, and now lives in Tokyo, Japan. He holds a BEd (Hons) in Literacy Studies from the University of the West Indies, Mona, and an MA with Distinction in Creative Writing from the University of Hull. His work explores the vestiges of colonialism and the effect of urban living on well-being and mental health via the immigrant experience. Versions of stories in this collection have been published by both *Wasafiri* (whose prose judges said his work was "vivid" with a "spectacular voice") and *The Caribbean Writer*.

Stories

FOR LEROY (COUNTRY) THOMPSON

I couldn't accept that silent visit to the hospital, from which you did not return. That was too quiet for you. So, I fixed it. I have you now going to see the ancestors on a brakeless market truck. You'd love that. It's the least I could do after you've paid for my English B exams.

O death, where is thy sting? O grave, where is thy victory?

The Holy Bible KJV, 1 Corinthians 15:55

The Devil's Horsewhip

It was a summery September day when he left the hospital. No. That was a lie. It was more a scorching piece of concrete, bringing a fresh wave of heat to his backside. Dennis, an English teacher on sick leave, was heading back to his place in Fuchu City. As he'd said to his wife T when they left Jamaica to go foreign, it would be a shame to leave the Caribbean only to perish in sun heat in another country.

'Jeezam, the place hotter than Jamaica noh true,' he said to T. 'Or is just me feeling the heat?'

And he had good reasons to enquire. He had just ended two weeks of hospitalization and the medication made him feel worse than his ailment.

In 2020, Tokyo was that kind of never-ending sweat stew. Could a place torment laka duppy? Picture roasting breadfruit in a blazing bamboo fire. It was a daily joke that the rain threatening to fall but then changing its mind. Even the Tama River—prone to flooding—sucked down to something resembling brackish mud in the once-sweeping riffles. In the same way, the usual deluge of people in the streets dried up. The entire country quarantined; people trafficked online instead until the internet crawled. But the cicadas, those raucous bugs, had just hit the annual crescendo.

The only peace for some people was that the kinmokusei were in flower. Those orange blossoms of the sweet olive trees hinted at the autumn cool. They hung from loaded branches like peeled persimmons put out to dry. And they smelled just as sweet. Other people spent their days in hiding. Curtain-twitchers. Trying to glimpse those who were brave enough to walk about in the 'Covid air'. The occasional funeral processions of hired mourners, trailing behind a giant taiko drum, were a welcome spectacle. The dreadful booms heard for miles put the death knells of church bells to shame. Not to mention obon; the cucumber horses and aubergine cows shrivelled up under that ripe sun as soon as they were put out to transport the natives' ancestors. The dead, as usual, were offered their favourite foods and clean water, that turned out to be an all-time favourite for stray cats and field crows as well. This was also when remote work came into its own. People dressed only the part of themselves seen on Skype or Zoom and spent an awful amount of time with the family. Of course, that was if they liked their family.

What had happened was this. Dennis had been feeling puny-puny for quite some time after going for his annual check-up. Some weeks later, a notification covered in red writing came from the doctor's office. It wasn't looking good for Dennis. Japan was big on feel-good vibes, so things like disclosing serious medical conditions were optional. Dennis with his presumptuous self let the people know that he wanted it straight. No cut corners. Now that he was called back to the office his heart was fluttering like a headless fowl. Doubt crept in. Dennis took a silent oath. 'Weh yai noh si haat noh leap.' If he didn't look at the notice it wouldn't hurt him. Like an ostrich and him head inna hole. Now only an ambulance or hearse could drag him out to Nakano to see the doctor. Well, that's what he thought. T rode him hard laka jackass a go pound to take himself to the clinic. Dennis couldn't win because for T, talking was like breathing.

T and Dennis couldn't be more different. If your dressmaker worked out of the church basement or shopped where the church drapes were sold, then you and T possibly posed in a back issue of *Good Housekeeping*. She was flawless to look at though. Her smile sliced her eyes into tiny lemon pieces, and they twinkled like sunshine trapped behind her lashes. Dennis' shirts hugged close to his midsection. Not a problem to him though. At least the buttons no longer floated above gaping slit cuts the way rotten pickney pulled down their bottom eyelids, stuck out their tongue and made silly faces. Besides, when people must look down to see you, eyes don't always fall on you. But even if Dennis and T resembled mother and son together, they both woke with a smile to greet each day.

Dennis loved teaching. T loved psychology. Maybe that's what brought them together, her curiosity and his logic. Despite growing up in the same parish in Jamaica, the two had met in the US. T's version of this meeting was that at a restaurant in Flatbush, her eyes drew to a pudgy 'country man' stirring his ice to cool his drinks and gyrating to a soca song. She knew only Caribbean people swirled their ice like the wrist and glass were mixing mortar. A story Dennis denied laka Saint Peter. That was ten years ago.

3

It was the morning of 1 September when Dennis dragged himself out of the house to go and see the doctor. But from he got to the train station, he could feel problems stalking him laka malevolent spirits. The first sign of trouble was a young woman cutting the queue. She came running through the ticket gates with tousled red hair, a spring scarf, and a factory-creased suit. A little overdressed for the weather, uneasy-looking, sweaty. Almost broke his shoulder with her big bag. She made her way down the escalator and onto platform number two; the sign above read: Trains Bound for Takaosanguchi/Keio-Hachioji. She darted right, head-on into the waiting queues, all the while adjusting her scarf and rummaging through her oversized tote. She fished out a cell-phone. Must have been vibrating. Then there was a flurry of finger pressing and the phone disappeared again. Dennis would have given her a piece of his mind, but people mostly apologize in Japan, irrespective of who the guilty party was. Such a thing rubbed off on you overtime.

He kept his eyes on 'Ms Red'. It was a novelty to not be the only one who stood out in the ocean of brown eyes and bowlegs for a change. He watched her hobbling over the yellow tactile paving blocks. She skirted around the queues, tripping over the tenji blocks then stopped behind a mother with a rosy-cheek baby peeking over her shoulder. She eyed the air-conditioned waiting room but seemed to decide against it. Appearance was everything in Japan. To sit would be to risk having a crushed suit to go to work. Plus, she was bursting with anxiety. The 'new teacher' kind of anxiety.

Dennis remembered his junior high school students. He was missing them. The aspiring kogyaru girls who couldn't wait to bleach their hairs and shorten their skirts in high school. They seldom participated in lessons. Even the over-bearing male language enthusiasts with the unusual mashup of Japanese and English: 'konnichi-what's up? (konnichiwa) and 'ariga-thanks (arigatou gozaimasu) and worse of them all, sumima-sorry (sumimasen). Dennis sucked his teeth and perished the thought of returning to teaching them.

Moments later the display board lit up red and the station guards started shouting instructions. The trains were delayed! Everyone panicked. Something had happened. Something terrible. The silence broke. Whispers of 'Jisatsu' spread through the crowd. On this of all the days, some poor soul decided to end things on the tracks. Probably one of the worse experiences for foreigners. Not that you saw the gore of remains being scraped from the crash site, but it was the urgency with which everyone moved on. It was how the sum of another human's life was measured in the simple message: 'Accident on the tracks. We'll resume operations shortly.' Cold.

An exodus to move from platform two began. Pair by pair, people made unison steps like the wingbeats of all-black carrion crows until they converged in a tight flock at the top of the stairs. 'Ms. Red', now a lone, red-crested cardinal trapped in the murder, jostled for breathing space. She darted side-to-side. Dennis tried to keep track of her but failed. A station manager stood centre of the throng, creating a Moses-effect for people to use both exits. He issued apology slips like an automated dispenser. These would come in handy when you turn up at work late. How else could you explain unpunctuality in such a time-conscious society? Dennis thought about heading back home but to do this again some other day was just too much to handle. He weighed walking across town to a station still in operation or having to listen to T giving him marching orders. Commuting on foot across town turned out to be the better option.

Dennis caught a jampacked express train from Chofu bound for Shinjuku Station, pressed up on a window, and he only got proper exhales during the time taken for half the cart to empty and twice as many people taking their spaces. At Meidaimae Station a crowd of people had to back into the train, helped by the hefting from a stocky passenger-pusher. He kept shouting, 'Tsugi no densha ni notte kudasai!' It was a plea for passengers to take the next train. A plea that was ignored. It reminded Dennis of the loader-man in every Jamaican bus park. Only difference, a loader-man was out to help himself. He would shout, 'Small-up yo'self mek smaddy else come pon di seat,' or 'One an' ready!' when even the blind could see that the bus was already overloaded. 'Damn nuisance.' The train didn't move for a while. The doors kept opening and closing. While all this was going on, Dennis looked out at a few window cleaners, suspended on the side of a skyscraper. Urban mountaineers scaling a sun-kissed glacier.

Then it happened for the first time. Dennis' eyesight became foggy. It was as if a frost appeared out of nowhere and the mountaineers disappeared. At Shinjuku Station the eyesight got worse. Dimmed lights smudged over his eyes just as cold fat smeared on plastic plate and spread worse with every rub. Dennis found his way around the world's busiest train station on instincts alone, thanks to the 'penguin march' that commuters joined at Shinjuku whether they liked it or not. He made his way from the Keio Line to the Japan Railways platforms. First, he was walled off on all sides by other passengers until he was in a tunnel lined with cold dispositions. Packed tight. Dennis, a frozen molecule in a block of ice. As they approached the underground walkway, a bottleneck formed. They squeezed. Undulated at both ends of the walkway like a lazy caterpillar. Up ahead the ice fractured, and people broke away in chunks as they emerged from underground into crevasses of the Japan Railways platforms. It was calving, powered by a network of incessant surges of travellers. People often flowed to the wrong places in these surges. The oversized numberings on the platforms were a lifesaver. How else could poor Dennis know to skedaddle out of the slipping ice, a literal tobogganing onto the platform he was being pushed past? But at Nakano Station it was pure problem. He could really use a loader-man then. Someone to haul him to where he wanted to go. Instead, he had to count paces to the atrium in the shopping district, turn right, walk two blocks, pass the Family Mart, to the clinic right across the road. These directions replayed in his mind until he arrived.

The waiting room was scanty. Dennis sat to one side, keen on giving more space than required for social distancing, or maybe he just couldn't see how far he was from reception. After he'd written what felt like a biography on all known relatives and given a blood sample, the nurse returned red-faced. His blood sugar had spiked to an alarming level. Later, he went in to see the doctor. The man had a face like a Japanese rock garden, one raked by the frown doctors make after many years of giving terrible news to patients.

'You're. Going. To. Die.' He counted the words.

Barbed English, like it was recovered from a dusty drawer.

'If no. Hospitalization. You die,' the doctor tried again.

'Does this death sentence have a name?' Dennis enquired.

The attending nurse pointed the doctor to the blood test results, almost as if to signal that he could share that information instead of playing 'death angel'. Then it was another long wait for the doctor to tell him that he had diabetes. He instructed the nurse to prepare documents for Dennis to go to the hospital right away. Then asked him if he wanted to be hospitalized. What did he expect him to say? 'No, I want to go home, take an aspirin and sleep it off!' The good in all this was that Dennis could be admitted to any hospital in Tokyo. He chose the Tama Medical Hospital. A hospital close to home. A hospital far from 'Doctor Doom'.

Dennis scrambled back to the Family Mart. There, he bought a phone charger and toiletries. He had strict instructions not to return home but to head straight to the hospital. He called T and laid the news on her.

'Look how you could be here and some'n worse happ'n?' she lambasted him.

'How about it if I get a second opinion before yo believe the worse?'

'What yo woulda tell mi?'

'T mi noh dead yet and if mi did dead wah mi coulda tell yo seh?'

'Stay deh man, tekkin seriousness mek joke.'

A warning message indicated the impending death of the battery. He promised to keep her updated and hung up. Then with the spirit of a Jamaican loader-man guiding him, Dennis made his way to the hospital. There he had a double dose of bloodletting and a Covid test—harrowing but mercifully brief. It turned out to be true. Dennis was diabetic after all. He was admitted to the Eleventh Floor, and it rained for the first time in a long while. It rained every day for an entire week.

Dennis watched the last slice of sunlight confuscated in a starlight blaze over the remains of the rain, puddled on the rooftops. He missed T. The days bludgeoned him and dragged, smeared a dry bloodstain colour across the cityscape. Every day he went to the ceiling-to-floor window at the end of the corridor to look down on the city. And at the foot of the building, some two hundred feet below, an ant march would always be taking place. From up so high it was as if the people made small pauses like insects greeting. Even from that distance it showed the locals routinely berating themselves, overemphasizing some menial accomplishment not worth a fly's attention.

His eyes would then return to a skyline covered in dusk. Utility poles were tohbas, wooden memorial boards, and the city a grey and spectral graveyard. The streetlights flickered in garish orange until they were as fully coloured pumpkins.

Dennis thought his wife kept him on a strict diet, but all that complaining was something he grew to regret in the hospital. They had him bird feeding between insulin shots. It got quite lonely for Dennis too, especially after T got off the phone at nights. Then he could only listen to the sound of small feet as they shuffled in the hallway. Young girls clad in powder pink garb disappeared in a flash like the spring Tokyo had lost that year.

On his bedside table sat a bouquet of wilting chrysanthemums. T had sent them in advance for their upcoming wedding anniversary. She was previous like that. A woman down the hall argued every night about Amabie, some mythical being that she believed to have predicted the pandemic. With his limited Japanese skills Dennis picked up that Amabie was part bird, part man and part fish and came out of the ocean and prophesied. Nobody listened. Now we were all being punished. Dennis scoffed at the idea. Jamaicans are superstitious but not like the Japanese. It was the little things. Take for example the pronunciation of the number four, which is the same as the word for death (shi) in Japanese. Different Kanjis mind you, but that don't stop people from dreading every four. Dennis' eye test on 4 September moved to the following week. Didn't bother him too much though, because it was on the Sabbath, and he had worship with T.

The man next to him snored laka untuned radio skipping through channels on a bad frequency. All put together, it was the definition of what Jamaicans called saltness. And Dennis was salt and miserable till the day he went home.

It was no surprise that a fortnight later Dennis was home on his first day picking a quarrel; questioning T laka police. A run-in with death would do that to most men. The need to question things became a new vocation for Dennis. He was out of his glass tower with its niggling slight pains of elderly snores and banter. The constant dings of the railway crossing, the Covid death toll announced over the community PA system, and the cat-scuffles left over from a night of mating and fighting was a stirring irritation down in Dennis' nether region that was bound to come out!

'T yo noh hot?'

'Yo waan know sup'n 'hot'?'

'Wah coulda beat this heat?' said Dennis, his voice so high that he sounded like a cicada bomb.

'Well, I was going to share something I found about how people with dementia are treated in Jamaica,' said T, all calm and smiling. She closed the laptop. Swivelled her chair until she faced him. 'Do you remember when you were young and older people would be dying and they started talking about all the bad things they did?' she said in a worried voice.

'Yeah-yeah, the wicked confess and then dead.'

'What if they weren't confessing? What if they didn't just die but...'

'But what?'

'Killed Dennis! Killed!'

'Really? That is the 'hot' yo talkin' 'bout?'

'Yes, mi blood a bwile! Uncle Sonny, Soldier George, Ms. Winnie, and whole heap-a other people might have been murdered because they were sick.'

'Of all that is happening right now, yo more concern with who kill Ms. Winnie?' Dennis said as spit sprayed from his mouth. 'Yaa the best yaa man,' he said in a way that tells you the word coming out of his mouth is different from what he was thinking.

'What's yo problem, Dennis?'

'Mi naa've noh problem inno.'

'No man, yo jus' angry all of a sudden soh.'

'Angry?' Dennis said, then sucked his teeth. It sounded laka when green plant'n touch hot oil.

'Get it off your chest. Whatever bothering you.'

'Yoh know wah, maybe mi angry. Maybe it bother mi seh after all the dieting and exercise mi still end up wid sugar! Is like one ant's bringing back poison to the colony and all other ants get poisoned. Smaddy in my family just spread sugar pon everybody. So yeah, mi angry. Mi angry when people think a craven mi craven mek mi get sugar. Nobody consider that it could be hereditary. Dem jus' judge yoh. Di fact seh mi have a date wid death and you…'

'What about mi? Say it!'

'Yaa worry 'bout dead people.'

'That's not fair,' T said with her voice breaking. 'You of all people know how much this degree means to me. You know about the relationship I had with Uncle Sonny. How could you say that?'

'Well, maybe mi haffi dead to so you can show some interest in wah mi going through.'

'Oh, so your "sugar" as you call it only affects you? You know, I've allowed you to mope around in peace because I knew you were feeling some type of way lately. I get it. Yo pride bruise,' said T.

She folded a tea towel, unfolded it and started at it again.

'Look at all what you did: you put distance between you and the lifestyle you grew up in, you played sport, diet, avoided drinking and smoking, only to still end up with diabetes.'

She bunched up the tea towel and tossed it in a corner. Dennis flinched but kept quiet. Her body shook as each volley of words escaped her lips.

'But brejin, you're forgetting how your A1c level was twelve per cent going into the hospital. That is now six point eight per cent. That's a gain! You're no longer taking insulin jabs. That's changed to oral meds. That's another improvement! You can reverse this disease. It's not a death sentence!'

She drew closer as one about to fight but no blows were thrown. Dennis listened without eye contact and rolled a single crumb between his finger and the table.

'But no, you're here feeling sorry for yourself. By the way, who makes your meals? Who ensures that you take your pills on time? And one more thing, you know why I've been so interested in these dead people and this degree I'm doing? With diabetes you're at a higher risk of developing dementia than other people. So, before you filth on what I'm studying again just know that it has so much to do with you than you believe.'

T turned and walked over to the corner. She stared at the crumpled tea towel, crouched down and gently cradled it. Then fold by fold she went at it again.

It looked like the eyebrows gathered rain and hung heavy on T's eyes. Guilt bowed Dennis until he was almost prostrated on the hot, wooden tiles. A few reed warblers skittered on the wall behind the apartment until a cat came and they all disappeared. The cicadas buttoned their high note as the evening signalled the day's curtain call.

Tokyo stopped for a split second.

A toilet flushed upstairs and the silence shattered. The two looked at each other. No words shared for a while. Just a discourse in the language of screwed faces and squinted eyes.

T finally spoke. 'You must be hungry now.'

Dennis hurried to get the words out. 'I waan hear the stories if yo remember dem.'

'You're sure?'

'Yes. But fix us a smorgasbord and get mi pills before yo start so you don't have to stop in the middle of it.'

'You're pushing your luck, mister,' T responded, moving towards the kitchen.

She returned with the items. Pulled the chabudai from the corner of the room, placed it between them, laid the snacks there and turned on the lights. Then she began.

Uncle Sonny came back to country by night bus. Nobody said anything out aloud, but I knew something was wrong. It was summer '96. I remembered the water at the parish tank went low and they had to open it to scoop out what settled at the bottom. The slugs, fattened by all that moisture, had eyes peeping out the size of grass blades. Snakes gliding from side to side made the black water tremble and the million frogs' eyes glistened in the blackness. It was a year of problems.

No wonder to this day I don't swim and when I'm near water where I can't see the bottom, it triggers my thalassophobia.

Usually when family coming from Kingston it's big fanfare. The three of us children; me, Ernie, and Michelle had work to do. Floor must clean. Curtains washed. Wood gathered in the old kitchen. And people from far and near know to come by the house because we would be keeping 'a little thing'. At least that's what dad calls it, 'a little thing'. But it was big things in Three Hills whenever we had anything at the house. We lived in the bush. As beautiful as it was, the sun seemingly showed its face after it was tired rolling 'roun everywhere else.

Ernie and Michelle went to stay with their mothers in Kingston. Me, being the child shared between mom and dad, had nowhere to go.

Mom and I had been pouring castor oil in quart bottles in the old kitchen when the dogs alerted us to the verandah. Dad had returned. With him, a wraithlike tall man sat on the banisters, waving nervous hands from a large dungaree jacket which enveloped him. He had dry, scaly ankles peeping out above a pair of scratchy sneakers.

'Still love Coronation bread?' he asked mom and pointed to a duffel bag beside him. 'This one just came out di ov'n.'

It was a five-pounder. You could see the half-baked centre through the checkered plastic bag. Just the way we liked it. As hot as the night was, mom pulled her buttonless cardigan at the chest and wrapped herself before approaching the man. 'Sonny?' I remember she whispered his name. Tears welled up at the corner of her eyes. But a joy shone from his honey-coloured eyes, and a dance-like jig started around his pasty lips. He then looked across the blackness. He still had the gentle voice and the puss eyes that were said to have all the women from country to town weak in their knees. Everything else about him belonged to a stranger.

His eyes flashed around to us again, this time walled-off by a single bulge in the centre of his forehead. The softness gone. His eyes made smaller by an inquiring gaze. 'Who fa lil bwai dis?' he said looking at me.

'You don't remember, T?' Dad asked with a chuckle in his voice.

'Mi gyal!' Uncle Sonny blurted. 'Why yo dress so?'

I was wearing one of Ernie's khaki pants and a big T-shirt. And I had used Dad's tailoring scissors to cut off the jerry curls at the beginning of third form in high school. I started dressing like that after an encounter I had with a horrible preacher. Dad being first elder at church meant us always having to entertain church folks. Pastor Johnson took over the Three Hills circuit after Pastor Davis died. He and his family stayed with us on several occasions until they were like family. Well, that's what I had thought. I was in front of James Avenue in the evening of the last school day before summer break, waiting on a taxi to go home, when Pastor Johnson horned me and said he was going to Three Hills. I wasn't one for free rides, but I know I wouldn't live it down if he should go by the house and I could have gotten a ride and refused it. Plus, it had started to rain. I went with him. He was his usual friendly self, as most preachers are. But things got a little strange after we passed Content Garden and turned off on the Gulf Road.

'Do you have a boyfriend?'

'Speaking as a teenage high school girl,' I said, 'this isn't a conversation I should be having with a grown man, let alone a preacher. Besides, it's none of your business.' He appeared embarrassed. We drive silent for most of the way after that until I noticed he went past Charles Town Road. Then I remembered that he always drove up to the little junction in Ginger Bottom, where you could turn for Lodge, turn up the big hill to Three Hills or continue out to Cascade, Labyrinth, Gayle side. I heard there's a big water park in that area now. Anyway, I didn't want to look afraid or vulnerable, but I wasn't naive, so I took out a literature book and feigned reading, all the while watching him from the corner of my eye. As we started ascending the big hill I saw him reach into his pants and whipped it out, start pleasuring himself while smiling at me. Thinking about it now feels like ants marching down my clothes. I flung the book in his face, popped the car door, and ran out in the rain. I heard him calling me back but, terrible as I was in sports at school, nothing could catch me. Back then, I had only seen myself naked. I felt so dirty. The rain was being spilt on the hillside in bucket loads but it only made me feel wet and nasty. It didn't cleanse the horrid feeling from my skin. It certainly didn't wash away what I had seen. When I got home and told Mom, Dad had to hold her down in the house because she swore that she was going to castrate him. It was the first time I saw my dad cry. We almost left the church. Pastor Johnson had to give Three Hills a wide berth but not before Ernie used stone and mash-out his car glass. That ordeal taught me that anyone can be anything on any given day.

I didn't like being reminded of Pastor Johnson but when I'm asked about how I dress, I usually tell people it's my style and that the world would soon catch on. So, it was the same answer Uncle Sonny got. I was relieved when he removed focus from me and brought up his niece in Maryland.

'Iz di siem way Avril use to dress til wi hear shi hav gyalfren.'

'Avril was just a chompo-nanny fram di day shi bawn,' Mom said between blowing out the tears that gathered in her nostrils.

'Tomboy Avril? Lawd shi strong like any man,' Dad chimed in. Then he took up the duffel bag and led us off the verandah, still talking about Maryland and dressing.

After just months of staying with us, we noticed some very peculiar things about Uncle Sonny. He didn't sleep. He was up all night talking, crying, singing, and laughing. Meals had to be served in certain colour dishes for him. He was afraid of the black scandal bag. And he had occasional quarrels and fights with people only he could see.

Don't laugh, man. It wasn't a good sight, seeing a grown man pick himself up one minute and the next he was being thrown down by the breeze and it and him wrestling in a banana root.

Mom said it was stink in Kingston that it was obeah that caused Uncle Sonny to behave this way. Apparently Castell, Uncle Sonny's nephew, said he didn't tell the whole truth about why Uncle Sonny had to leave Kingston. Yes, he was sick, but the real reason was that out of the blue, he kicked a man at the restaurant he was working. The man promised him he was the last man he was ever kicking. Castell thought they were planning to kill him but after he quit his job, stopped showering and walking about they realize it was obeah. Dad didn't care. 'Obeah or not, I'm not going to Canada leave him ya,' he would say every time the topic came up.

Before leaving for farm work in December, Dad took Uncle Sonny to the doctor. His sister in Maryland sent money for him to have his check-ups and to ensure that he had clothes and food. Uncle Sonny wouldn't go in to see the doctor. When we asked if he was afraid, he pointed at two children in the waiting room eating ice cream and cookies.

'When people come doctor dem fi get ice cream and biscuits,' he said, wailing like a child and telling us he was going home. He was always saying that: 'I'm going home, I'm going home.'

Now when I recall these memories, I realize that Uncle Sonny didn't even know his age sometimes. He had all the classical symptoms of dementia. Early onset dementia to be exact. I often wonder how lonely it must have been for him that we didn't understand him.

When Dad left for Canada, Uncle Sonny still came for his meals at the house. When anyone tried preventing him from entering especially Dad's side of the family, he had some choice words for them:

'If Johncrow can go in deh wa fi hinder mi?'

Nothing could stop him entering. Nothing, until after that black welcome mat was bought. On one side there was big, bright yellow writing. It seemed to attract the dogs which then gifted it in payments of fur and fleas. Mom woke up on the morning of my birthday, 8 January. Dusted the mat. Flipped it over and set it back down on the landing step of the verandah. Uncle Sonny wouldn't cross it. He thought it was a hole dug for him. Pearl, the lady who wash for us, sometimes would take his meals to him. We didn't want him to karate us in one of his fights by mistake. Pearl wasn't afraid of him. She spoke to him in a firm but kind voice.

'If yo no change yo wayz bad things bound fi find yo and I'll be dere to witness it.'

Uncle Sonny always smiled and listened to Pearl. I think he had liked Pearl.

In just a few years after coming country we started seeing less of Uncle Sonny. His mind had become a clothesline between his ears. Some days it got on like a good wash day. The laundry went up and the sun and breeze prepared them for the folding later. Other days, like bad luck, the line would burst. Depending on where the break occurred, you had the laundry spilling to either side or everything rushing to one side—rushing in the past or the future. Either way, when a perfect wash was thrown in the dirt, whoever had it to deal with couldn't make head or tail of the pile of dirty clothes.

Dad was going on farm work twice a year now. Mom started travelling, too. It was just us kids mostly at home. Uncle Sonny had started wandering again. He'd be gone for months. People sighted him as far as Discovery Bay. We heard that his fights with the breeze had become more violent where even his blood was spilt. But I know wicked people would jump at the chance to hurt him. Uncle Sonny didn't have the kindest tongue and people knew they could only catch trouble if someone had seen them do it.

Then we didn't see Uncle Sonny at all. We would have to get a search party going to find him for his doctor's visits.

It was on one such search Pearl found him faced down in the ramshackle house he was born in. All the time he was saying that he was going home… that was where he went.

I think someone could have knocked him down and left him for dead.

Hear me out first. I have my reasons.

Around the same time, in neighbouring Petersfield, we had another suspicious death. There was this World War II veteran called Soldier George living a solitary life for years. Then out of nowhere he started mourning his wife. He didn't hear well. Like others, I presumed that it was caused by the heavy artillery shelling in the war. Ruling out that fact, and the occasional bouts of bunions that had him testing his weight like a Woodcock, Soldier George probably would have outlived us all.

We heard that he was de-branching an ackee tree on his property. Fell out the tree. Knock his head and started talking pure gibberish. All manner of foolishness. 'Yes sir! 'Turn right! Turn left!' and 'Fire in the hole.' But strangest of all, he mourned for his wife, whom he claimed to have died the very morning he fell out the ackee tree. Miss Meryl, his wife, died before Soldier George even came to Petersfield.

It was one thing for his mind to be running away from him like when river come down. People would ignore him. But when he brought his imagined war to passing school children, all that changed. The schoolers had to skip the stone grenades he threw, and soldier crawl pass his yard in the gutter. We knew he would catch trouble. It wasn't long after that the white Ministry of Health bus came to Petersfield. They had a straitjacket and bad injection for Soldier George. He would go to Bellevue, come back later calm as a lamb then kick off again. And this kept repeating until his son had to come down from England to see about him. Maybe he was trying to get him over there so that he could get the kind of treatment that could help him. But Soldier George was in a world by himself. When he couldn't manage any longer, his son had to get help to tie down Soldier George on his bed. This to me made the old soldier feel like he was captured, so all the defensive wounds his son sustained was nothing but him dispensing his training.

Pearl would help with the cleaning and cooking. After about a month of trying, Soldier George's son had to go back to England without him. Pearl stayed on like a live-in helper. The health authorities kept check on Soldier George, but it appeared they had done something bad to him while at Bellevue. Every time the bus drove 'round to George's yard his head would go off. The men and their injections would have to parlay safe passage or engage in an all-out war. I wasn't surprised when we heard that Soldier George passed on. People suspected a bad injection put him down for good. We all went to see them take his body out of the house when the hearse came. For a slim man, Soldier George was so swollen we thought he might have burst at the touch of being lifted out the sunken bed. The skin, blackened at the hands and feet, signalled that he was bound to the bed. The sight broke many hearts. That man was a national treasure and to see him go out like that caused many to question his death. Poison? Torture? Bad injection? The list went on but with his son not wanting an autopsy, Soldier George was buried, and everyone moved on. Nothing came of it.

Soldier George's son cut ties with Jamaica for good. He gave the old house to Pearl and told her that when she was getting married, he would give her a gift. Something people say to unmarried women whose chance of ever walking down the aisle is slim.

First, Uncle Sonny. Soldier George followed, and like dominoes toppling over, Ms. Winnie's time came. Ms. Winnie was a big shot in the area. She had a shop at the foot of a clearing in Charles Town District where the road to Petersfield and Three Hills connected. It was the only shop for miles. She enjoyed good business. She was also a big political activist. A fact she broadcasted in pictures on her walls, in the political paraphernalia she wore, and the contents of her testimonies at church. 'Is far Winnie coming fram,' Mom would tell us. Apparently, she started selling soup on the roadside and worked her way up in society. We could either believe that or what her critics had to say about her. 'Shi get all wah shi hav' lying on her back.' A saying they had to point their mouths to the ground and say or they couldn't 'trust' any goods at her shop.

Ms. Winnie was a tall, light-skinned woman with long straight hair and two bright, full eyes. She could easily pass as white. She had two children, Ralston and Faye, who took the charcoal colour of their father Mass Buster. He and Dad went on farm work together. Ralston and Faye were in the same grade as Michelle and me, but not in the Common Entrance Exam class. They weren't big readers, something else they took from their father. Mass Buster's big daughter, Hyacinth, and her husband Trevor lived with them. Ms. Winnie took sick after one of her politician friends lost his seat in a general election. All Mass Buster's farm work money and her savings were tied up in the politician's campaign budget. She took it to heart. Her mind got clouded, the way an untrimmed lamp wick blackened its shade. Nothing was ever clear again; till the day the light went out of her eyes.

Ms. Winnie's decline in health was swift. She lost control of her bowels, something that became a coat of paint for the shop walls and an unwanted gift for passersby. This all got to Mass Buster who drank and chased frock tails in Ocho Rios. He wasn't around much after that. It was Hyacinth and Trevor who took care of Ms. Winnie. Hyacinth was a good Christian girl, very active in her church. Even if she wanted to abandon Ms. Winnie, her conscience wouldn't let her. Trevor on the other hand was very ambitious. He wanted to control the shop. But the health authorities gave them notice to close the operation more times than there are days in a week. I think he couldn't wait for Ms. Winnie's eyes to close.

Thoughts of speeding up the process must have crossed his mind with all the money that went down the drain for him. Then again, Hyacinth and the children wouldn't allow any harm to come to Ms. Winnie, though. That was until she started confessing.

Before day broke each day for about a week the tied-up Ms. Winnie would talk some things that shattered the hearts of everyone in earshot. One September morning, bright and early, we were heading back to school. Ms. Winnie gave out a shout:

'The leftover soup weh di skool pickney dem drink, a mi bath water length'n it! A soh yo tame customaz!'

I was so glad that I didn't eat from anyone. But Michelle and Ernie almost vomit-out their insides at the thought of lapping up the free soup. Her children stopped coming to school. Hyacinth and Trevor worked overtime, tying down Ms. Winnie's mouth to stop her from saying all those things. But Mom told us she had a lot more to say when we were at school during the days. She explained that when they had to remove the gag to have her fed, she chatted her life story and it was hell for them to tie her mouth again.

'Tuesday, shi seh di burnt endz people love to beg from the jerk pan wasn't alwayz pork or chikin. Missis, all di missin' dawgs en-up inna dat jerk pan.'

Michelle and Ernie looked at each other and started bawling.

'Wenzdeh,' Mom continued, 'Shi rob church collection. Shi seh shi jus' show di big note, tek di change fram di collection plate and kip buot money.'

'Criminal!' Michelle blurted out, 'Hyacinth mus' kill har now, you know she is Jeezas right han.'

'Lawd Jeezas, Turzdeh woz 'bout stone inna di rice, flour and cawnmeal fi bring up di weight. Shi wet di saltfish fi mek it heviyah. Freeze water inna di chikin back so people pay mo' money fi less meat.'

'Mi did know shi not fair, but mi did tink iz back shi back di scale,' said Ernie.

'Mi to, caaz ongle shi could si har scale face,' Michelle said, motioning in the air at how Ms. Winnie would flip the scale with a flick of the wrist.

'But iz Fraideh unu fi hear,' mom arrested our attention again.

'Wi noh waan hear.' Michelle and Ernie covered their ears in protest.

Mom wasn't laughing now. It must have been the worst thing Ms. Winnie uttered to cause mom to look that serious.

'Shi seh shi get Ralston an' Faye fi tek ada pickney book an' pencil fi carry go obeah man. Shi use dem fi put down people pickney and elevate fi har. Dem get bath a Mada yard to but dem chil'ren kyaan tu'n duck aafa nest wid a pupa laka Busta.'

'Zas Christ,' Michelle cried, 'Mi Junior English book.'

'Yeah man,' Ernie snickered.

'A nuh like mi nyam jerk dawg laka you.'

Mom gave them both a look and they stopped mouthing off at each other. Only just a few bad eyes and giving each other their backs remained.

Apparently, the obeah man story was the last straw with everyone. Mom told us that Friday morning a big crowd went to burn down the shop with Ms. Winnie in it, but she was already gone. Did someone beat them to it? Hyacinth? Trevor? Mass Buster? Or was it just natural death? Mom told us she was bruised all over. The residue of vomit and sputum caked to her face. The curtain rods used to restrain her, almost cut into the flesh.

It bothered me for years that she was treated badly and now in my research on dementia I've learnt that most recollections in this so-called death-bed confession may not even be a person's own memory. It could have been something she heard, read, or even thought about doing but didn't do.

Looking back now made me realize that only Pearl wasn't too perturbed by the situation. She just stood inside the shop waiting for service while the commotion to remove Ms. Winnie's body raged. Other people's hatred for Ms. Winnie seemed to have waned but I couldn't get a read on Pearl's behaviour. She was just minding her own business as if nothing had happened.

'Now, today September twenty-seventh, 2020, even if you think there wasn't any foul play with Uncle Sonny's death or Soldier George's death for that matter, Ms. Winnie's death must be troubling to you. Tell me it's not a stretch,' said T, stabbing a finger laka dart in a square on the garbage collection date calendar that hung on the wall above her desk.

'I'll reserve my deductions until after I've examined all the evidence.'

T punched him on the shoulder. Dennis pretended to be knocked over and chuckled. He really wanted to say the colourful things he would have done to Pastor Johnson if he could get his hands on him now but all that would be meaningless.

Besides, he didn't want to dwell on it after hearing T's past about how much she hated discussing it. So, he just repeated 'I need to examine the evidence.'

'Anything you say Sherlock Crumbs,' said T, as she brushed the mess he made on the chabudai.

She took the empty tray to the kitchen.

Before you could roll over in your bed, autumn came and went. It was like going to sleep one night and waking up next morning to find that the sun had fallen on the hillsides. The green hills covered in haze. Something laka the springtime yellow sand from China. Time stopped. The leaves, nature's traffic lights, flashed in amber and red. The trees shimmied out of their dresses and got ready to stretch their bony arms into the grey skies. Rows of hot beverages filled streetside vending machines. Scarf season had come. And with it came flu season as well. It was also the season of pocket warmers and throat sweets. But for Dennis, those first couple weeks back home were mainly a time of deep reflection. The stories T shared came back to him every day.

At nights—when Dennis was alone in the dark with his mind—the fear of death swarmed him the way Maybugs would crowd a bulb until no light was seen. After the thoughts of death found a good strand of hair to land on, they mated, laid, and hatched. Then the little nymphs chewed themselves free until they fell on the broken dirt of Dennis' heart. When the worries in his heart bugged him, he screeched in his sleep. The neglected and despised people living with dementia in those stories made sleep quite elusive. Those worries were like cold weather cicadas. They burrowed deep into the nether region where conventional cold formalities and pretense couldn't silence them. Then as the season changed with just a glimmer of warmth, they surfaced and nagged the same way most cicadas you've heard weren't necessarily a new brood but oftentimes mixed with re-emerging crooners.

Dennis hadn't gone back to work but a week and already the return was proving difficult. Missed a couple trains. Forgot to pack indoor shoes. Managed to forget taking his pills. The worse thing though was having to deal with frequent urination. That's all metformin did, pull urine. After T had words with Dennis' doctor about how metformin was recalled for causing cancer everywhere in the world except Japan, he was put on another generic drug instead. Less side-effects but it was yet another piss-inducing pill. Dennis dreaded the thought of urine leaking from his bladder in its own time or to be going around smelling renk laka ram tiger.

The second week of work, T had to shore up Dennis. He had the 'new teacher' anxiety. A short visit to the hospital and the world had moved on. People he knew had new interests. Big city people who were always on the go, had no time for the sick. His students matured overnight. Dennis felt sorry for himself. And T was all he had. She gave him mantras, post-it notes and optimized his phone with sound and vibration settings along with the annoying note alert tone coming on laka bad feelings every twelve o'clock.

'Your ancestors survive the voyage across the Atlantic.'

'Yes,' said Dennis, prancing in the mirror laka male fiddler crab trying to catch a mate.

'Slavery!'

'Yes!'

'And so-so food.'

'Wait, what?'

'Well, that's what we have for breakfast.'

'The salmon and chicken breast,' Dennis sighed.

'Don't worry about it, I'll go to the store later.'

Dennis went back in the mirror to continue getting dressed. T watched in admiration as he continued mouthing the mantras and paraded his good mood. He gathered up all the jewels in the family chest, wrapped them all in the hem of his undershirt. Extra precautions for the leaky bladder.

'What's that?' T asked with a quizzical look on her face.

'What? The man-diaper technique?'

They both laughed.

'If I don't do it dis way, the smallest drop of urine will feel like di pants front soak.'

T was forced to agree with him. Cold weather had that effect on damp clothes. Soon factory fumes would face the searing cold in the violent way striped eel catfish murmurate to dodge predation. And for miles, all the eyes would see was that silent cover of white crochet as if sheet-web weavers got news of flood and took to the air.

Dennis worked through the remaining second term. Aced his performance assessments. Made it to winter and the third term without incident. There was even talks of him getting a promotion. He should have been happy. But T's stories of how people with dementia lose themselves and were treated plagued him.

Would he go out like dat? How would T cope with it all? She deserved so much more—he couldn't expect her to care for him like a child. He should be positive but it was no good—he just couldn't.

The thoughts in Dennis' head were further amplified by the winter blues. They made him think only of the worst. He would grin to appease T but when alone, he was a man at war with himself. But each time he would carry-on laka this, wallowing in self-pity, he would remember a mantra and chuckle. The note alert for his pills reminded him that he always had someone in his corner, and he fought on. It was this glimmer of courage he took with him to the winter training to close-out the school year.

His company had them meeting at a community centre out in Nakano. The seating arrangement was sparse, Covid protocols were the order of the day. Dennis didn't expect much. It was a half day of work. One of those mundane events where one would attend to ensure the day is covered for the sake of not losing a coin from the already meagre salary.

But it would turn out to be an eventful training after all. Lo and behold, the presenter was none other than the 'Ms. Red'.

This must be a sign. What were the odds that they should meet like this again?

Dennis and his depressive self knew meeting this woman again could mean trouble. Sparks were bound to fly. He kept giving her nothing but bad eyes throughout the entire meeting. When they had a break he was first to leave the room. He headed straight towards the little park that laid in stark contrast to the concrete slab that scarred the scenery. A picturesque pond sat close to the landing of a descent of steps that formed a cosy nook beneath skeletal branches of maple trees. Trees that were the envy of spring, summer, and autumn. If it wasn't for the two old men kotched on the low retaining walls at the top of the steps feeding a small kit of pigeons, and a tiny turtle crawling over a mossed rock, Dennis would have been alone there to have his meal. He had just pulled up the collar of his covert coat, and whipped out the veg stir fry and quinoa lunch T had packed for him, when the sound of boots came sauntering down the steps behind him. His phone rang. He hurried to shut it off and took a quick look behind him. He sucked his teeth at what he saw.

'Hey, where are you from?'

Dennis answered.

'Wow, you're far away from home.'

'Not quite. T's my home.'

'T?'

Dennis lifted his left hand to reveal the wedding ring.

'Do you always lead a conversation with your wife?'

'Habit, I guess. It prevents confusion.'

'Or is it to make a girl know what she's getting into?'

'Nothing of the sort…'

'Kristina Appleton,' she said, extending a hand to shake.

'Dennis,' he responded and chuckled.

'What's so funny?'

'You don't want to hear it.'

'Come on say it.' Kristina punched Dennis on the shoulder the way T would.

The old men had seen enough. They left and took the birds with them. She was playing a game Dennis knew quite well. He knew that when a magician dangled one hand in front of your face, you should be looking to see what the other hand was doing. He knew the interest in him wasn't so-so. But sometimes playing along could reveal everything.

'Are you sure you want to know what I'm thinking?'

'Spit it out already, Dennis.'

'Kristina Appleton? OnlyFans?

'What? You didn't!'

Now they were both laughing, and Kristina was playfully thumping Dennis like they'd known each other for ages.

'Thought you were a gentleman. Clearly, I was wrong.'

'Maybe I was just getting back at you.'

'For what?'

'For my shoulder.'

'Those baby hits?'

'Nope. Your big bag at the train station some months ago.'

She looked puzzled as if nothing connected. Dennis described the suit and scarf dressing. And how the train had stopped running. Her eyes widened. More laughs and a string of apologies followed. She was a long way from creased factory suits and tousled red hair. Her hair was now in a neat bob but still red. The blush of her cheeks made the whiteness of her skin more pronounced. It gave her a delicate look. Even though it was obvious that she owed the winter for that nice tone.

'It's almost time to go back,' she said while looking at her watch.

'Hmmm, meeting again.'

'Don't be so enthusiastic,' she said with so much sarcasm it gave away that she was American.

'Whereabouts in America are you from?'

'I'm a New Yorker, D.' She slashed a grin with it and continued, 'I know I can come off as brash but I'm a sweet gal.'

'Good to have a name for the face.'

'Same here, D. Heard about your performance assessment last term. Good stuff!'

There it was! The reason for the sudden interest. Was this a test? You could hardly trust anyone because foreigners came to Japan and forgot all the liberties they enjoyed in their home countries. They became so complicit with blatant disregard for basic workers' rights for even the smallest recognition of being set over another foreigner. As harmless as it looked, the small talk could have far greater meaning than putting a face to a name. If that wasn't the case, why weren't there any witnesses? An email could accomplish the same thing but why would you establish a paper trail if you wanted deniability for having a conversation?

'Thanks, Ms. Appleton.'

'No, call me Krissy. I think you should be on this side of the company.'

'No.'

'Why not?'

'Maybe it's the last bit of dignity I have left, and it will have to be prized from my cold hands.'

'Whatever, I know it and you know it to be true. Who knows, maybe next term it will be you who is doing some of these trainings.'

'Next term?'

'Yes. And I'll be there to witness it.'

What was that she just said? Where had he heard it before? Witness it… witness it… oh yes, from T's story.

'What do you say to that?'

'Next term is not here yet. We'll have to wait and see.'

'Be positive,' she said as she rose from her stoop, brushed off her coat and turned to head back to the meeting.

A few steps ahead she looked back as if to say, aren't you coming? Dennis motioned to her to go ahead. When she disappeared beyond the steps, Dennis had his meal and headed back himself. The meeting ended earlier than scheduled. They all hurried out of there and headed home. Kristina was trying to find Dennis again for a chat, but all Dennis wanted was to share his evidence on the cases. He found it funny how he had forgotten about the stories and now the answer was just given to him like that. He was convinced of who the killer was. It all made sense. Why was this one person present when Sonny, George and Winnie died? Dennis found Pearl to be very fishy. He got to the station. It was crowded. Noisy. The warm room was packed. He stood next to a platform bench. Tried calling T but she couldn't hear a thing he was saying. Icy and lazy winds were dragged in and out of the station behind each train. And the chattering wouldn't permit it. He decided to send a text instead. This is what it said:

Babe memba d lady in red I told you about some months back? Met her again 2day. Conversed about a lot of nothingness but it wasn't entirely fruitless. She said something she said, 'I'll be there 2 witness it.' Who was around when Uncle Sonny, Soldier George and Ms. Winnie died? Pearl noh true? Lawd fi Pearl confession would draw crowd...

(BOOP! BOOP!) KMT! Battery almost dead...

What was he doing? None of this didn't make any sense. Now he was the one worrying about dead people. Pathetic! He should be focused on the new job. That is if it is real. You can't tell with these people. Then again, how could he celebrate with his predicament? Why even bother? How could he be this excited and sad at the same time? Thinking about these stories was like walking over his own grave. Wasn't this a fate he was being pulled towards?

Dennis pressed and held down on the backspace button. The cursor wiped the first few words. He released his thumb. He battled with the thought of sending the message and just wiping it away. His hands trembled. He mumbled one of his mantras. He forced a smile. He believed he could fake it and bury the overwhelming doubt that was floating around his head. He fought. But he lost in the end. The thoughts made a nest in his mind. He pressed his thumb again. The cursor began darting backwards. Character by character until the message was cleaned away. Dennis took a deep concentrated breath and watched the misty exhale joined the alien world of wind-carved snow hugged to rooftops and anything that didn't move.

Dennis looked around. It was a cold day in Tokyo. No. It was a frigid and spiteful day. Could a place bite laka morgue's freezer? Picture the crisp air wending through every alley like a furry puss tail. It jumped through open windows. Wrapped around naked necks. Pressed up against the legs of high school girls, scratched till they're bruised. In 2020, Tokyo was that bitter slab of ice. People naturally did the jig of exchanging weight from foot-to-foot. And only pigeons queued. On car hoods with running engines. And next to the kitchen vents of restaurants and ramen shops. They perched there in hopes of catching their fill of warmth to survive, filling their lungs with breaths of wintry knives.

The first few local trains rolled into the station and ate the crowd the way hungry caterpillars nibbled their leaves.

In holes first, then entire sides until only veins remained. Dennis decided to take up residence in the warm waiting room and waited for the rush hour crowd to be squeezed-on home. At that hour train cars were sardine tins. Express trains whisked by with a sound like the making of Kakigori. Powdery snowflakes, now frenzied, bulleted through the air as though they were violently scraped from a block of ice. Where the wheelsets slammed on the rail joints, you couldn't tell them apart from an old hand-crank shaved ice machine. And the evening sky was a flavourless bowl of plain mochi. But all this was happening outside the room. On the inside, Dennis was joined by an elderly geisha. His eyes quickly glanced at her. She had on an indigo-dyed hanten covered in pine leaves and butterflies. And under that short winter coat, a kimono adorned in pink plum blossoms and bamboo. She sat intently on the edge of the seat protecting a small bouquet of narcissus and unopened plum buds.

The door slid open! A man looking as if he was scraped from a pavement in the Kamagasaki slum lumbered in. The woman made room for him to pass between them. The plastic around her bouquet crinkled. She caressed the flowers back to silence. The man apologized in hand gestures and head nods. The fingers gripping a bottle of lemon soda had nails striped in grime that went up to his face to form a clasp with the other hand, only to reveal eyes reddened by insomnia or some cheap liquor. He had on about seven layers of clothes. All raggedy. And a funk, thawed by the warm air, started filling up the small room. The man made his way to the back glass where there was a poster advertising The Great Buddha of Jorenji Temple. He turned away from the poster, leaned up against the glass and started bawling. Not the manly pained sniffles but wailing. After a while he apologized again. This time he vocalized his remorse in a deep and broken voice. The woman smiled at him as if to say it was okay. He then reached inside the pile of clothes he was wearing and retrieved one of those hand-written temple seals. Ran a jacket sleeve across his face once and caught all the tears. And faced the poster again.

Then came the all too familiar pattern of two bows followed by two handclaps. That was Dennis' cue to get out of there. He recognized the Shinto prayer. He had no problem with it really, but he regarded the prayer man the way he did any other 'religious recruiter', thinking that he too intended to accost foreigners and have them pray to Mt. Fuji and donate money. The man started wailing again. Whatever was wrong with him must have been serious. The woman tried consoling him with her bouquet of flowers. And while they spoke, Dennis slipped out.

Dennis walked to the other side of the platform. With every glance he made behind he could see the woman still trying to help the man. He was pacing back and forth. Beyond the yellow lines and then back to a safe distance. He was her problem now. Dennis went farther away. He ended up at a section of the platform that was free of people but marked with bird droppings. He scoured the beams above and skirted the poop. In the joint of two beams, a barn sparrow's nest sat precariously. There was no nesting board to catch the platform manure that had piled up below. But like a problem sewn to the feet laka shadow, Dennis left one trouble only to have found another one.

He noticed that each time a train came whistling through the station, the little sparrow would swoop down and try to attack it. The flapping wings and shrieks of the bird, in an uncanny way, reminded him of a time a pudgy little boy had dropped candy on the tracks and was adamant to retrieve it. He wore an oversized jacket covering his hands, and they flayed as wings as the tantrum consumed him. Dennis learned the purpose of this bird's madness when he peeped over on the tracks to see that an egg had fallen out of the nest.

The eki-melody signalled the oncoming train. The train music helped to keep the river of people flowing through the train stations. The bird stopped preening. Skittered from side to side. Perked up its wings and started its maddening cries. The tension heightened. It was inevitable that something bad was going to happen. Dennis even tried shooing the little bird to stay in the ceiling. But it floated above the rafters and dropped. Dennis tightened his behind and closed his eyes. The train horn blared, and a gush of cold air slapped his face. And like a fast earthquake rattling a boardwalk, the tracks argued with the passing train. He opened one eye to find the bird still sitting on its perch. He exhaled, looked around to see if anyone else was concerned with the bird. The little critter had a small following. Some cheered for its resilience and others begged it to stay alive. But no such attention was given to the man at the other end of the platform. Even Dennis had forgotten about him.

Dennis closed his eyes again but this time he was so affixed on the plight of the bird that he could hear its heartbeat. The Horlicks-brown plumage striped in coffee seemed so close he could reach out and touch it. He tried. But this time when the little bird left the rafters, the train wasn't so kind. A burst of feathers wafted about as dandelion seeds in flight. The train horn resounded, and Dennis opened one eye again to see that the little bird had not moved. He must have been tired. It was all in his head.

By then, the crowd on the platform had shrunk. There was an express train coming next and then a local train would stop at the station. Dennis thought about catching that train. He walked back to the centre of the platform where he could get off the train at a good spot to transfer to the Keio Line at Shinjuku Station. He met the pair from the warm room again. The woman was no longer stately and calm. She was all muddled from dealing with the prayer man. The heart-racing feeling came over Dennis again. The prayer man was now inconsolable. Station workers had joined the woman trying to calm him, but the mention of police made no difference. It ticked him off worse. He threw the bottle in his hand, not at anyone specific, but the behaviour made everyone back off. He glared at his pursuers and inched slowly backwards. Backwards and closer to the edge. The station workers held back. He hugged the bouquet of flowers close to his chest as he stopped close to the tenji blocks. Finally, they were able to grab and hold onto him. He appeared agreeable as he apologized to the woman, and they tried to hurry him off the platform.

The eki-melody came on and again he heard the wind from the oncoming train. The prayer man wrestled free from the two guards and rushed towards the track. Dennis stretched his arm out and opened his mouth wide, but no sound came out. It was futile. He closed his eyes and turned away. Bam! A gnawing screech followed. Shards of shattered glass became seashells being rolled by waves. They tinkled back and forth between frantic feet, which created a cadence identical to the flattering of a heart in crisis. Every piece of glass was a little mirror of the thoughts and imaginations that were going off in Dennis' mind. A jaw-locking pain slapped him in his face. Sharp and electrifying like gag-reflex, hurt like biting through the tongue. His pores expanded, flushed with cold sweat. The air quickly changed from its odourless winter freshness, carrying first a tinge of burning metal and plastic, then sickly sweet molasses, and finally raw and acrid as if pickled in dead kelp. Then it was all muffled sounds and no smell at all. Dennis shrank smaller and smaller within himself as if he was buried alive or underwater. Suffocating. Gasping for air. Thumping his chest. The geisha, her clothes peppered with fragments of flesh, fell over and scooted backwards on her palms and backside, almost knocking over Dennis. The alarms went off. People hurried and gathered, screamed and turned away. An orchestra of sirens and fragmented announcements increased in tempo. Yellow jackets and helmets entered the tracks. Blue screens were erected. That message announcing a human accident on the tracks came again. An exodus from the train station shaped up and moved out. Dennis was caught in the flow. He tried looking for the kind geisha, but everyone wanted to be out of there.

On the road, the long line of taxis got busy. As the adrenaline subsided, Dennis saw a scene from the accident for the first time, an image of the flowers wreathed through the man's ribcage. He grabbed his chest and tried to stop his own heart from coming out.

Dennis caught a taxi across town to Shinjuku Station. The images kept replaying in his mind, along with the feathers and the dandelion seeds. How could a bird's life seem more important than that of a human? He leaned his head against the window and looked at the world going by. What was the man's name? What bothered him so much? How would this change everyone who witnessed the accident? What about the geisha, was she alright? Who would pay for the loss of revenue for the rail company? Stopped at a red light, he noticed the roots of a ginkgo tree growing through the pavement. Dennis traced every strand that found a crack in the concrete and burst through. This powerful display of unexpected life brought some solace to his heart. He closed his eyes and as the lids touched, hot tears seeped out and trickled down his face. The taxi driver eyeballed him through the rearview mirror. He said nothing. The driver tuned his radio. The melancholic dirge of Katsu Shintaro's 'Otentō-san' swelled cloudlike in the backseat and then rained on him. Behind closed eyelids, Dennis revisited the times T tried to cheer him up. The value of staying in the light was so important at this point. He promised himself not to be so prickly and stubborn. He wanted to be a more appreciative person.

Dennis felt less judgmental of the locals who moved on quickly when someone died. He finally realized that they were not entirely being cold the way they process death, but it was more about choosing to live. It was about drawing a line and telling yourself that no matter how life beat down on you, you wouldn't go past that line.

That was where you fight.

'Hai, Shinjuku-desu!' The car door popped open to the cold city.

The glassy pavements had begun reflecting a neon glow. Shutters on café windows slowly rolled up. Together they were like eyes lifted from phone lights—curious eyes welcoming arrivals. An inquisitive gush of wind tried to whisper in unsuspecting ears but didn't wait for answers. It had the attention of a kitten at the end of a laser pointer. It rattled the wagasa handles in the umbrella stand sitting outside a convenience store. It howled and made the slow-falling snowflakes swirl as disturbed doves. Then it hung from the back of an ambulance slicing the late-evening traffic and left. Everything and everybody were either going, or waiting to go, someplace. Most people moved along predetermined currents the way schools of fish lined up head-to-tail. Those behind izakaya windows sat motionless as aquarium fish do before being fed. The snowflakes returned, noiseless. They stuck to the windows until they were scaled over as blinded eyes. Talk about being alone in a crowd.

Whether it was burning or freezing, this was Tokyo.

Dennis entered the train station. The overhead heater in the head house laid in wait, surprising passersby with a merciless downburst as if Karakkazes were tipping off a mountain. It howled like wind-dried winter daikons, curtained around farmlands. The nonstop touch of IC cards at the ticket gate clicked and clacked as loose cypress shingles on a hilltop shrine. Escalators hummed, trains can-crushed their way in and out of the station but nobody made a sound. The occasional announcements, the opening and closing of train doors, the hissing hydraulics and the train engine's throttle and acceleration became a rhythmic blend. It kept passengers awake.

Dennis got off the train and popped into a convenience store.

'Irasshaimase!' yelled the staff. It was almost strange. The first human voice for a while yet it didn't warm the ears nor free the tongue. It was mechanical enough to be lumped in with the self-checkout system. Dennis silently grabbed his groceries and headed home. His walk was accompanied by tyres squishing over slushy ice and the notice of streetlights with urine-coloured snow at their feet. He got to his door and was about to insert his key when the intercom crackled like an old vinyl record:

'Where yo going at this hour?'

'Yo waan give me heart attack?' Dennis said.

'Yaa rude bwai,' T continued.

'Why yo not in bed? Yo deh ya frightening people laka duppy.'

T laughed and made a nasal sound mimicking a duppy.

'Our neighbours must think we a mad people,' said Dennis while opening the door.

The door slowly opened, and the bright yellow light poured over the steps. Dennis schlepped through the narrow door with his bags and allowed it to close on its own. Every inch of light, like lava, cooled and turned to basalt.

'Duppy?'

'Raah!' T came running through the living room with a blanket draped over her head.

She jumped onto Dennis and they both went crashing into the getabako. A few shoes tumbled and fell on their heads. They sat on the floor guffawing and rough-romping laka puppy dog.

'Yo feel yo strength t'night?'

'Yo know how long I've been waiting for you?' T replied.

'Yo gwine be di death of me,' said Dennis as he gathered the shoes and placed them back in the cupboard.

T carried the groceries into the kitchen with Dennis following close behind her. He probably was waiting for a bag to fall from the way T used one hand to drape the blanket around herself and the other to string the bags on her wrist and forearm. A stack of carton boxes grew out of a corner. Dennis pretended not to see the delivered items.

'Told you I was going to have a good Christmas this year,' said T as she announced to Dennis what was in the boxes with a nod of her head and pointing with her mouth. Dennis responded first with a grunt of some sort but then grinned gleefully when T gave him a wide-eyed stare.

'Ketch di Christmas spirit if yo know what good for you,' she mouthed off.

'I'm in di spirit man, call mi Faada Christmas.'

'Now that yo have di right attitude, a can show yo what I got.'

Dennis reached for a box. 'Eh-eh!' T interrupted him and pointed him to the bathroom.

'Get the city off a yo,' she continued while pinching her nose.

'Okay then boss,' Dennis murmured. He then tried to enter the bedroom.

'Just step out of all of it and leave them by the bathroom door, I'll deal with them,' said T as she hurried him.

A soapy, warm bath was waiting for him. Hints of eucalyptus and bay leaf were carried on the steams floating about. Dennis stepped inside the tub and slowly slid himself into the herb stew. He reemerged for air with some colour in his cheeks and a pleasant look on his face. He breathed the aromatic blend in his bath and exhaled long and hard. He closed his eyes and not long after fell asleep. He was brought back by T's gentle nudges a while later.

'Come before yo waterlog,' she said.

'Was I out for long?'

'Not too long, hope you enjoyed it.'

'Can't you tell?' Dennis flashed a smile.

'Well, it's a long while you haven't smiled like this.'

'Thanks love, I truly appreciate this.'

'Wow, courtesy, and gratitude. Who's this man and what have they done with my Dennis?'

'Yo have jokes… clown girl.'

'Mi a duppy and clown girl now. What that say about you that tek mi up as wife?'

'Mi a must ringmaster.'

The two burst out into laughter again. T handed Dennis a towel.

'Let me get a quick wash-off and come,' said Dennis.

He came out of the bathroom to a living room draped in pepper lights laka black wist on guango tree. A little Christmas tree was set up in one corner along with several wrapped gifts.

'How long was I really asleep?' Dennis asked jokingly.

'Hahaha, it was an easy task. You like it?'

'Like, no. Love, yes!'

T patted herself on the shoulder. Dennis thought she wasn't going to make all that has happened earlier this year ruin Christmas. She didn't ask Dennis about the train accident or how he was after such a terrible day. She must want to get all of this sorted out. She must want him comfortable.

Later they sat around the kotatsu table. Dennis had chicken soup while T cut his toenails and oiled his feet. Dennis felt pampered. He just kept on smiling. He wanted to help with the dishes, but T wasn't having any of it.

'Just sit yo ringmaster behind, right there and let the plate spinner do it,' she said.

Dennis picked up a few nail clippings, brushed off the kotatsu table and tried looking busy. It was difficult for him not to do anything. The lights and tree brought back many childhood memories for Dennis.

'Yo used to get your future read from egg white a Christmas time, T?'

'No sah. Dad always seh dem deh a obeah bizniz.'

'Backside. Forgot that yo family religious!'

'Very!'

'Then how yaa string up Christmas tree and yo religious?'

'Look ya, Christmas tree no have not'n fi do wid anything,' T said pointing with the knife she was washing.

'Amen sister,' Dennis replied.

'If yo must know, I usually look forward to licking the baking tins come Christmas.'

'Me too. Going for wood and watching my uncles prepare the animals for the feast was at di top of my list too.'

'Well, the white beard man preparing our feast this year,' T quipped.

'Who, Santa?'

'Nope, The Colonel!'

'Blow-wow. You were able to get a KFC order?'

'A bizniz me mean,' T said in a confident voice.

'Yo miss yaad?'

'Sometimes, but we a yaad people. We can mek yaad anywhere we are.'

T finished cleaning up the kitchen and sat beside Dennis.

'I know you had a rough day,' she said.

'It's okay…' Dennis started. 'You don't have to deny it.'

T cut him off. 'Whenever you're ready to talk about it I'm here but tonight I have better use for that smart mouth of yours,' she said.

She opened her kaftan and revealed that she was wearing nothing underneath all this time. Dennis swallowed hard. There hadn't been anything intimate since his diagnosis. He hesitated but T gently brought his head to her bosom and caressed his ear.

'What, it has been so long, you forgot what to do?' T teased Dennis.

Things got so hot inside, it rivalled any fireside but outside, a heavy snowfall started. Snowflakes appeared like pinpricks of sunlight on a black sheet until everything was blanketed in a rich lather of foam.

The next morning Dennis was awakened by Christmas carols and the scent of cinnamon and nutmeg. The drapes were drawn, and sunlight volleyed through the mesh curtains and formed shadows laka ants marching inside the room. He yawned and stretched. Through his squinted eyes he searched for T in the kitchen, but she was nowhere to be found. Dennis lifted himself off the futon, much in the way that a yogi performed the downward dog pose. He then lumbered to the bathroom. Still no T. Before heading back to bed, he went to have a look at the intercom. Lo and behold, T was outside shoveling snow laka man doing bolo work.

'Hi, hi lady what yo doing?' Dennis called out.

T walked up to the apartment, dusted her boots, and brushed off the snow gathered on her clothes. Dennis went out to meet her. T opened the door and cold air squeezed past her to get inside the warm room. Dennis had to take a speedy retreat. T saw him cower from the little cold air and laughed.

'Yah man, back up yo'self! Why yo coming to fatigue me?'

'No such thing. I just don't want the neighbours think mi in bed while you shovel snow,' Dennis replied from behind the door.

'Yo too love worry what people think,'

'It's not really a worry but yo know how people stay.'

'Well, if it's any consolation, I'm wearing your clothes so they goodly think it was you out there.'

'Hmmm.'

'What, only a real nosy person would look and see that it was a taller person out in the snow,' T jeered.

Dennis kissed his teeth and held the door handle so T couldn't come inside.

'Wait, where was all this energy last night?'

Dennis got offended and let go of the door handle.

'I know that would have done the trick,' said T, bursting inside with the cheekiest grin on her face.

Dennis said nothing. He just marched back into the room and slid back under the covers. T tickled him through the blanket and fought to see his face as he was stifling the laughs. When she finally got the blanket from over his head, she saw that he was checking emails on his phone.

'Not happening! You're disconnected from all that. We're spending this break. Just the two of us,' T demanded.

'Okay, done!' Dennis closed the phone and threw it down.

'Turn it off.'

'Off?'

'Yes, off!'

'Off, off?'

'Yo want it mash up?' T asked.

The intercom rang and T jumped up and rushed out of the room. She came back with more boxes.

'More gifts,' Dennis enquired.

'It's a copy of *Mastering Diabetes*, a lunch kit and a water bottle for work.'

'That couldn't fit into one box?'

'Different sellers mate. Leave online shopping to the professionals,' T explained to Dennis.

'I hear you.'

'I'm sorting you out for next term. We'll be better prepared to function with this disease and reverse it in short order.'

'I know I'm in good hands.'

'Then hand over the phone,' T reminded him.

'Okay bossy.'

'I'm Duppy, clown, bossy, this, and that. Make up your mind!'

'You're my sugar plum.'

'For the next couple of weeks, I'm your happy manager. That means nothing to do with work or anything to do with stress.'

Dennis and T spent the break cooking together, watching old movies and playing board games. At night they watched the glow-in-the-dark stars on the ceiling and reminisced about their childhood. They exchanged spa days and enjoyed each other's company. They even went out a couple of times. Once for a music presentation at a mall and another time to see the illumination displays near the Fuchu train station. Things were looking good. Dennis was in a happier place. He was planning future outings with T and was becoming more focused on getting better. He worked out with T, took his pills on time, and even bought a stationary bike.

A few days before Christmas they got a late-night call from Jamaica. T answered the phone. It was Dennis' brother on the other end of the line. Dennis watched as T's smile slowly went straight and then limped downward.

'What is it?' he asked with his eyes popping out.

T held the phone to her chest and the tears came rolling. 'T?'

T began bawling and gasping for air.

'T, waap'n?' Dennis asked.

'It's your mom.'

'What, is she in the hospital?'

'No.'

'No? Give me the phone, T. Give me the phone.'

'She passed away, Dennis.'

Dennis laughed in disbelief. Then he went silent. He dragged open the screen door and stepped into the backyard in his pyjamas alone.

'D!' T called out. 'D, come back inside.'

Dennis stooped in the snow and mist and silently wept. He wanted to scream but he was so adjusted to life in Japan that he kept his noise to himself. T went out with a blanket and covered him, begging him to come back in with her. His feet turned purple and the colour left his lips. He had become numb. It was T who was feeling everything for him. She pulled him back inside and left him lying on the floor and went to fetch warm water. She had him sit with his feet in the basin and kept rubbing his shoulders and back. Dennis just sat there lifelessly gazing, his hands interlocked at the fingers and his lips sealed tight laka lockjaw.

'You're not alone. Stay positive,' T whispered in his ears every few seconds.

She held him close and kissed his face. Stone-cold anguish plastered across Dennis' forehead every now and then, but it melted back to nothingness just as it would show up. He grimaced as he struggled with his thoughts but each time the vein bulged in his temple T would kiss it away. An hour or so later he spoke.

'Is it a crime for me to be happy?' Dennis muttered.

'No, you deserve to be happy,' T replied.

'Death just a follow mi so.'

'No, it's not.'

'You don't understand. Death has been chasing me all my days.'

'I don't like when you talk like that,' T complained.

'Nobody cheats death and live long enough to speak of it.'

'You know what, I get it, you're grieving,' T said as she seemingly surrendered to Dennis' negative talk and self-pity.

'It's too much. A just feel like... a just feel like to end things sometimes.'

'You can't do that.'

'Why not?'

'I need you. It might be too early to say this, but mom was getting old this was bound to happen at some point.'

'Doesn't change anything.'

'Not even the fact that I need you?'

'I'm no good to anybody now,' Dennis screeched through his teeth.

'You're good to me. To us,' T fired back.

'Don't bother 'bout us, you're better off without me.'

'Not you and I. Us!' T said pointing to her tummy.

T got up in a flurry, knocked over the basin of water and almost slipped. Dennis caught her but she flashed him off and ran over to the kitchen sink and began crying again. Dennis wanted to go to her, but the water was spreading closer to the futon. He quickly threw a towel on it. He removed the chair and basin. Then slowly went over to T. She was inconsolable. Her body shook as she bellowed out her pain. She kept pushing Dennis away until she was too weak to fight, and he managed to lock her in a tight embrace.

'When did you find out?'

'It was supposed to be my Christmas gift to you.'

'I'm sorry,' Dennis whispered.

'I had it all planned out and now it's wrecked.'

'No, it's not.'

'Move man, yo just bitter and angry so,' T criticized.

'I'm really sorry.'

'I'm hurting too. It hurts that your mom won't see this child I'm carrying.'

'I know.'

'Can't you just stop for a minute?'

'I can. This changes everything too,' Dennis assured her.

'Don't bother sorry for me and this little one. If you're not serious about living I'm as good as being on my own.'

'Don't say that.'

'Why not? Your flip-flop isn't going to cut it. You're either gonna be here for us or not.'

'I'm here. I'll always be here.'

'What, until your mood changes or something bad happens?'

'I can do better. It's just that I've been taking blow after blow. It's overwhelming.'

'I take those with you. I feel them too. Stop acting as if you go through anything alone.'

'I know we go through it together, but things are always happening to me.'

'I get that but this thing with death has got to stop,' said T.

'I wish I could explain things better to you.'

'Just tell me why you're so fixated on death. Don't try, just say what's in your heart.'

Dennis sat on a chair and rubbed his hands. He had so much to process. He couldn't believe he was going to be a father. With his diagnosis and all, having children was far from his mind. He didn't realize that the way he reacted to every displeasure made him look weak. Deep down, he knew these irritations didn't warrant him romanticising suicide, but he had done it so often that it became second nature. Dennis had kept his fear of death to himself for such a long time. He didn't share it because he hated being ridiculed. He stopped rubbing his hands, held up his head and said, 'No matter how what I'm about to say may sound silly, just listen and when I'm done maybe we both will learn something from it.' T tried to respond but he stopped her by pointing at his ear—a signal for her to just listen. T sat down beside him and allowed him to empty his heart.

'I guess I should start at the beginning. A little boy from my community named Leroy drowned in the White River. After his death, his friend Bruce lost his mind trying to convince everyone that death was after him because he was meant to die that same day. Had he gone to mango bush with Leroy he would have suffered the same fate. Eventually, death found him right where he was hiding. By then he was grown but death never forget who was owing. This was riveted in our minds that death was spiteful and is something you cannot cheat. When I was young too, I had my own run-in with death. A madman attacked me, my friend Markie, and some girls down by the same river where Leroy drowned. I don't know if it was luck or something supernatural, but to this day I cannot see how we survived the ordeal. We narrowly outrun the cutlass that day. But still, one by one everybody who fled the cutlass-wielding madman wasn't so lucky the second time death came knocking. Even a white woman who just happened to be in the community on the day got marked for death as well. Then again, maybe her reason for visiting on that day made death put eyes on her.'

Dennis crossed his right leg over the left at the knee and rubbed his hand over a faint scar line that encircled the heel. And for a moment he went silent, staring meaninglessly at the pepper lights hanging on the wall. T studied his face and kept silent, too, almost appearing emotionless. She was outwardly reticent about what was going on in her mind but inside she was countering every one of Dennis' superstitions with scientific evidence and every doubt with hopeful words.

Dennis started again. 'Death has a way of lying in wait like devil's horsewhip and when you least expect it, dig in yo flesh or wherever it can hitch on to you.'

T may have realized that with all the sayings coming out of Dennis' mouth he may not be open to reasoning. So she seemed to resolve to beat him at his own game.

'True,' she agreed with his utterances like an echo.

But was she waiting for a window to give him some superstitions, too?

'Once you're marked for death, yo done for. No matter how far you travel, just like how the prick from the devil's horsewhip will scar yo 'kin, it's the same way you're reminded that yo have an earlier date with death than most people.'

T nodded. 'That's one way of looking at it.'

'What yo mean?'

'Well just as how you're sure that a death curse exists, I'm positive there's a remedy.'

'Remedy?' Dennis scoffed.

'Well, you believe that people who escaped a near-death situation are cursed and hounded by death all their lives.'

'Exactly!'

'Alright, that is true but so is the fact that new life brings an end to death!'

'Mi don't follow you,' Dennis blurted with his eyes all squinty.

'Life follows death, and the cycle is complete.'

'So, you're saying that mommy's death and this baby will bring about an end to what plaguing me?'

'Yep!'

'It can't be that easy.'

'It was never hard to begin with. Besides what is death against a mother protecting her family? Pretty soon this pumpkin will swell broad enough to hide you behind it,' T said pushing her belly on Dennis and forcing him to smile.

'Yo sure this isn't just you trying to cheer me up?'

'Nope, I'm no clown girl today. I'm serious. By the way, you do know that devil's horsewhip is a miracle bush and only gets a bad rap because of its thorny appearance and that awful name?'

'Not a blasted miracle!' Dennis quipped and looked at T as if she was talking nonsense.

'Don't get me wrong, I know it is an invasive plant and while it may not seem to have economic value to some people, it is a big thing in Ayurvedic medicine. Even our common fowls would feed on the plant in the backyard, and you know fowl can tell the difference between good and bad plants, right?'

'I didn't know that!'

'Not only that, but this plant provides a vital object lesson. Just as you mentioned its bur-like qualities about how it attaches itself and follows its host, I realize that our memories that stay with us aren't always there to frighten or bring about some apocalyptic curse.'

'Boxcover, yo dropping knowledge, psychologist!'

'Oh, stop it.'

'No, no please continue.'

T blushed, seemed to collect her thoughts and start unpacking every detail like judo moves against every negative thought plaguing Dennis. 'No matter how hurtful our experiences are, we survive them every day we allow our loved ones to help remove the thorns. It's a matter of perspective, you can either give your experiences a bad rap by calling them awful names or find the good in them. You not only survived your past, but you've thrived, and you get to share in many people's lives. That's what I take from the devil's horsewhip. We're all attaching ourselves to the people we meet and share our lives with. Will our lives hurt others or heal them?'

'That was a mouthful,' said Dennis as he rubbed his heel again.

'Made any sense?' T asked.

'You never not make sense.'

'Yeah, but did it make you look at your experiences any different?'

'Well, I think with how you spin the devil's horsewhip what I get is that I can choose to be the devil, the horse or the whip,' said Dennis before a thunderous belly laugh.

'Well, if that's what you got poppy show. Please don't foo-fool like yo pa little one,' T said holding and looking down at her stomach.

'Di amount of thorns me have I must be a porcupine,' Dennis said with more gut laughs.

'Dennis clear off! Good to see that you can still laugh,' said T as she walked out of the room.

'I'm just messing with you, man. Doc! Don't go doc. You hit the nail on the head. I might have to start paying you for sessions. It's that good.'

'Don't patronize me. Besides you can't afford me,' T said and closed the door.

After a short while, Dennis heard T laughing inside the room. He went to find out what she was laughing about.

'What sweet yo so?' he asked after sliding the door open and peeping in.

'Your brother sent a recording of the death announcement of mom that went out over the radio. I know it's no time for laughing but I couldn't hold it in. Listen to it for yourself.' T handed the phone to Dennis.

Dennis listened to the recording about three times and sucked his teeth. His face twisted with embarrassment.

'What did the man say about wash belly? Tell me what it said, man,' T jeered at him.

'Not'n no go like that,' Dennis responded.

'Yo not laughing now? Laugh, man!' T insisted.

Dennis went out of the room singing: 'Rumour dem a spread.'

'And her wash belly Den-Den,' T said mimicking the radio announcer's baritone voice.

'Mi don't name so!' Dennis shouted from the living room while T continued laughing.

Dennis and T attended his mother's funeral over Zoom. T announced the pregnancy then and during the repast, all the conversations were about her.

'How China?' one family member asked her.

'Close enough, but for the one-millionth time, we're in Japan,' Dennis answered for T.

'If yo was here mi boil guinea hen weed give yo fi get rid of that sugar,' an elderly woman said, with her face right up in the camera.

'Why yo never boil it for mom?'

'Shi had her own medicine, and she live a full life,' the woman said while turning to garner support for her argument from others.

'Alright medicine woman,' Dennis teased.

She was hurried out of the frame for others to chat up the foreigners.

'How little chopstick?' another person enquired.

'Don't call me blasted pickney no chopstick!' T demanded.

'The boy is doing well,' Dennis answered again.

T got up and left the frame.

'Hormones?' someone else asked.

'Maybe just bathroom,' Dennis assured them.

He then warned them to be nice and not to make trouble for him. They chatted about old times and laughed among themselves. T eventually came back and joined the convivial atmosphere. In that moment, Dennis felt the cycle of life was in complete harmony. It was evident that as people they were more than just a collection of their past experiences. While they drew little droplets of memory from the well of the past, recollections were already getting murky and racing downstream before a thought could settle. It was a strange alchemy, like trying to carry water in a basket. But they had hopes. Hopes for the future even though they might never live to see it. It didn't matter. They made bold promises for when they would bless their eyes on the new family member who was making his way into the world as an ancestor was going out. The old medicine woman likened it to a mango falling off the old tree to make mulch at the root for the young bud that will spring forth.

They signed off Zoom amidst a hail of best wishes and hearty congratulations. Dennis turned to T with a bright smile hanging big and wide from ear-to-ear laka one freshly opened flu mask. He got up quickly and acted as a crutch for her. T was out of shape laka when snake swallowed egg—a shiny, Jamaican red racerlet ready to be bottled up in rum as pain medicine. Still flawless to look at. But was that enough light for Dennis? Enough to prove to him that even though death was known to attach itself to everyone like a shadow; if given a little sunshine—something to love, work at, and hope for—people chose life over death.

He had a strong feeling that T would make sure of it.

Then again, fear wasn't something that would just vanish laka smoke. It was a dark thing carried 'round inside a person laka the bones of dead family members, a revisiting blackness as dread and terrible as night.

Bunka Bat and Sour Orange

Morning; a shrill whistle from a pigeon's wings broke the silence. All the other birds in the city took to the air. A million feathers applauded the break of day. Circled. Then the sky rained bird feet on the metal roofs.

Bruce dragged himself out of bed. His eyes still wandered in the labyrinth of his dreams. Before his feet hit the ground, he began a series of bone-cracking stretches and face-twisting yawns. His morning pandiculations resembled an ugly exorcism. He sleepwalked, stretched, stiffened, and shuffled across the termite-assaulted wooden floor until he got to the window. He paused and scratched at the bed lines furrowed on the right side of his face. With one finger he parted the drapes and listened out for rain. It was a beautiful morning. Not a cloud in the sky. A fat cat scaled down from a nearby rooftop, stretched, and sprawled out in a warm patch of sun.

A few housekeepers hurried along Dewsberry Avenue. The music of their feet and the subdued greetings squeezed through the teeth were all too familiar a song to Bruce—country women without agency who left their family behind and toiled in the house of the bourgeois. He was reminded of his mother. People were out walking and enjoying the morning air. Just a few paces from his vine-covered gate, an old couple could be heard buying fruits from a street vendor. The man seemed agitated. He kept raising his voice. By now the entire street was privy to their conversation. Apparently he was telling the vendor about a dream he had but it sounded like the woman kept correcting him. Maybe it was a made-up story. Who knows? Who cares? It was human interaction. Bruce craved interactions.

'No Baron, nothing go like dat,' she said and added, 'It was Milo tea yo must dida drink caaz no Milo is yo favourite tea?'

'Aye Elvie, mm-hmm, you talk it den since a fi yo dream!'

Baron flailed his hands and stormed off. His shoes clacked on the concrete pavement and then crunched over the loose gravel in the driveway next door. 'Drama queen,' Bruce muttered with a delicious grin of mischief plastered across his face. Outside was calling him. He felt the urge to go out and have the sunlight dance across his face.

His cellphone vibrated behind him. He made a rapid turn to attend to it, caught his arm in the drapes, and dragged down the entire rod. So much for keeping quiet. He knocked off the picture frame from the dresser, shattering the glass on the floor. Shards lay strewn across the faces in the photograph like droplets of rain. It sent an ominous feeling over him. His forehead beaded with sweat. Old people said that a dead person's picture faded after a time but there he was, bright as day. Braces, pimples and a plastered arm—evidence of a lifetime of tumbles. The small boy stood next to two other boys and a girl under a coconut tree. Bruce grabbed his phone, pressed the home button and the screen lit up: *7:00 Saturday, July 7,* Siri announced.

He dropped it and backed away into a corner. Bruce slid down the wall that caught him until he was atop fragments of plaster that had peeled over time and littered the floor. All the joy and life he felt earlier drained from his face. He had a wide-eyed stare as if he had seen a ghost. The sound of his heart pounded in his head until he lunged forward and brushed away the splinters with his bare hands. Bruce grabbed the picture and yanked open the dresser drawer to hide it, but a cricket ball came rolling out to greet him. He paused. Why was this here? Another ghost from his past. The side facing the sudden interest of light gleamed in shellac brilliance while the underside shadowed an erubescent sun-drenched glow. He slid his fingers over the fading red topcoat, the unravelling quarter seam, the few dents in the cowhide, and the smooth hemisphere, which all coalesced into what was once a pace bowler's dream and a tail-end batsman's worst nightmare.

In his hand, it felt a little over a quarter of a pound and it just sat there, dull and soundless until he held it up to his face and caught a whiff of the ageing leather. Then it began to speak to him. He could hear the crack of willow and cork laka bamboo shattering in the harsh Caribbean sun, the deflated cheers following a dropped catch, and the chinks and clips of a cannoning cricket ball on a petrified pitch. Memories propelled at him fast and again he was bowled over in terror. Still, the unravelling seam refused to speak. Its brokenness haunted him. The old Dukes ball reminded him of his friend, who played his last innings in the game of life several years ago. Bruce had those memories of him, knocked far out of reach like hitting for a boundary set beyond an agoraphobe-unfriendly, empty, and forgotten cricket field.

Today the boundaries were rushing infield.

Ten years ago, today, Leroy Brown drowned in the White River.

After feeling embarrassed from breaking one of his memorabilia, Bruce picked up his phone hoping he had not destroyed that too. He had a notification. He went back, stood at the window, and listened, @*MindMarshall Retweeted: Therapy quotes aren't free therapy, you'll pay for it eventually.* It would have been better the phone was broken. Then he wouldn't have known about that dreadful tweet. He hated therapy. It meant going outside. He hated that too but today he had a four o'clock appointment with Dr. Marshall. The sessions were paid for months in advance, but given the dreadful start to his morning, Bruce didn't want to spend the entire day alone.

He took his time getting ready to see the 'MindMarshall'. In the end, he only fitted a pair of sunglasses over his tear-drenched eyes and threw a trench coat over his pyjamas. 'Mi know di dressing don't mek any sense, Leroy,' Bruce said out aloud. Yet, he was alone in the room. 'But dis iza special coat, nobody gwine si mi,' he shouted again. He made for the door, slapped his hand on his forehead, and returned to fetch a bunka bat and his cricket ball. The ball went in an inner coat pocket and the bat was tucked close to his armpit with the coat wrapped tight around his frame. Needless to say, he had a strange walk with all those accoutrements padded on his person. He waved goodbye to his pictures and he was out the door.

Bruce took a deep breath and marched down the street. He ignored everything to the sides of him, not that he could turn side-to-side at will. He faked normal as best as normal could be, even turning up his nose, as uptown residents would, on the street food shacks serving that 'eat it before it eats you' cuisine. But he was hungry and deep down he longed for the boiled crab and peppered shrimps. He walked for hours through pathways with more shadows than people. It was high noon when he got to Dr. Marshall's office. The sun, that summer-fruit, ripened and fell on the other side of the concrete jungle. It smeared a juicy golden stain on the topside of the western skyline. The city now blurred in sepia hues was perfect for Bruce to slip inside the office unnoticed. He also hated being a spectacle for the amusement of people who needed not to see the likes of Dr. Marshall.

The moustachioed and hoary-headed shrink sat in wait at his desk, eyes buried in his notes. Dr. Marshall's belongings were piled like a dump: a leather satchel thrown on the floor keeled over onto a suit jacket. A pair of dusty brogues on a heap of old newspapers. He was a brilliant therapist but a horrible human being. He once ordered a psychiatric evaluation and prescribed antipsychotic medication for a woman who had panic attacks. The source of her problem was that a lizard had jumped on her and her husband was locked up in prison and was about to come home. Dr. Marshall didn't care for superstitions but a lizard jumping on a Jamaican woman meant she was pregnant and there's no way she could explain herself to the absent husband.

'Mr. Parry, please have a seat,' said Dr. Marshall with his head still down.

'Dutty bongl,' Bruce muttered under his breath.

'How are we today?'

'Don't know 'bout you sah, but it not looking so good fi mi a tall-tall.'

'Sorry to hear. I would take your coat but it's probably best suited on your back.'

'Figet 'bout the coat, a having problem wid Leroy.'

'Oh, one of those episodes.'

'A think every screw loose inna mi head!'

Dr. Marshall finally looked up at Bruce. He saw that he was trembling and that there was more white than black in his eyes. 'The sofa, then?' he asked. Bruce moved towards the oak leather chaise lounge by the window and eased onto the plush leather without making a sound.

'I spoke to you about the attachment you have with objects from your past.'

'Kiba yo mouth,' Bruce barked. 'Mind yo upset dem.'

'Upset who?'

'Leroy,' Bruce whispered.

Dr. Marshall couldn't hold back the laugh after Bruce pulled the bat and ball from his coat. But Bruce was dead serious.

'What, you thought this would get you on meds?'

'Wa dem seh, notn beat a trial but a failure no true?' Bruce asked, then added, 'Mi sick bad-bad.'

'No, you're not. Man up, Mr. Parry!'

'Maybe mi need fi walk wid a lizard fi yo tek mi serious!'

'Mr. Parry, it is my professional assessment that you need human connections.'

'Like di art therapy session you hav mi doing wid di bag a ol' piipl dem?'

'Come now, don't be like that. Let's talk, Mr. Parry.'

The office was silent. Bruce got up and went to the window and just stared into the nothingness of the oncoming night. Another wasted session. Wasted just as the time spent painting fears to the soothing sound of the metronome to calm anxiety. Another one of Dr. Marshall's grand ideas to cure him without medicine. The metronome didn't soothe Bruce at all. The clicks haunted him, grated on his nerves like the unending drip and echo of water in a well.

Bruce wished things could go back to simpler times like the summer of '88 when he first met Leroy Brown and Ewan Haye in the seventh grade at the Newstead All-Age School. That year Hurricane Gilbert devastated Jamaica. School was out for a while and they had plenty of time to be boys in the wild; bird hunting, fishing, and playing cricket. Bruce loved cricket. They played in the street and the smoothest and straightest piece of road was in front of Mrs. Gloria Johnson's yard. She didn't want the boys trampling her garden and she had a few mongrel dogs to remind them of it. Still, the boys would go there to play whenever the family was at church or out shopping.

Bruce carved bunka bats from the coconut branch, Leroy picked the young sour oranges for cricket balls, and Ewan shaved slender guava sticks for the wickets, all found on Mrs. Johnson's land. That was how it was done for a long while until Jeannette, Mrs. Johnson's daughter, caught them at the front of the yard one day pulling down a coconut branch. Jeannette used it to her advantage to join the game. They had two choices, let her play or deal with her mother.

'Hey thief, what ya doing?' Jeannette called out from behind her window.

'Iz just a coconut branch we taking to make a bunka bat ma'am,' the boys chorused.

'Ma'am? It's me big heads, we go to the same school,' Jeannette said as she laughed.

'Oh, iz you, big mouth,' said Bruce. 'Iz only a coconut branch, what inna dat fi steal?'

'You're the one with the big mouth. It's not even a branch. It's called a petiole.'

Ewan and Leroy laughed at Bruce and there, a bitter hatred started between him and Jeannette. When Ewan would ask Bruce why he hated Jeannette so much, he would tell the story of the cuckoo bird that pushed the eggs out of other birds' nests and left one of theirs. He believed Jeannette was a cuckoo bird that would scatter their nest.

Mrs. Gloria Johnson was a horticulturist with more books than the orchids she planted. To Bruce, Jeannette and her mother were more bookworms than earthworms, preventing them from playing cricket on the good stretch of road in front of their yard. Mrs. Johnson wanted them nowhere near her precious flowers, but it was the only straight piece of road in the community that gave the boys sufficient time to scramble for their wickets when a country bus screeched tires around the corners at either end of the street. Jeannette was bossy and she made it clear that cricket couldn't be played in front of her yard if she wasn't playing.

After several days of dodging the dogs and Jeannette's big mouth, Bruce had no choice but to make her the new 'bothie', taking over from Leroy, the odd player on the two teams. They also brought many wild orchids in coconut husks to show Mrs. Johnson that they had a green thumb as well. Together, they transplanted all the orchids and hung them in fruit trees, and out of harm's way. It wasn't too long after, the stretch of road became their cricket field.

The outfit grew. Jeannette the bossy tomboy and a band of barefooted youths playing cricket. On a good day a full eleven on both sides would play. Soon after, the low-laying petioles and sour oranges got scarce, and they needed new equipment for the game. Jeannette suggested getting golf balls at the Upton Golf Course in Exchange, about two communities away from where they lived. Walking to Upton was fun. The gang enjoyed crossing over the White River and filling their faces with mangoes. They would storm across the new metal bridge that replaced the wooden one destroyed by Hurricane Gilbert. It was a good adventure to go to Upton but after all the torture they went through playing cricket with golf balls, Bruce and Jeannette weren't on speaking terms for a while. They only got back to talking after Jeanette was gifted tennis balls at one of her church raffles and the cricket matches started again.

In the eighth grade Jeannette suggested that they all try out for the school team. Ewan and Bruce were chosen, but Leroy was still too small to wear the cricket pads and no girls were allowed on the team. That was good news for Bruce since Jeannette didn't get to play but Leroy was lost without them. He wasn't allowed to travel with the team when they played against other schools and he was too ashamed to attend the home games. The street matches had stopped. The boys were playing real cricket and had no time to remove and replace their wicket at the behest of the horrid motorists. Jeannette took up track and field and a liking for Ewan and by the ninth grade Leroy wasn't seen much at school. Ewan spent all his free time with Jeannette and cricket practice kept Bruce busy. They all forgot about Leroy.

One day, on his way back from Upton, Leroy got trapped in the White River valley. It rained upstream and the jaws of the river stretched until it swallowed the bridge. He didn't know. He had crossed earlier without any trouble. So he went running with the hope of his feet echoing across the bridge. By the time he realized that there was no bridge, it was too late. The greedy river had space to swallow him too. He was found tangled in the bulrushes, clinging to his bunka bat and with a sour orange in his pocket—the only friends with him at the end.

Bruce blamed Jeannette. He thought every time she made a suggestion, something bad would happen. To him, Leroy was the egg that got thrown from the nest. Ewan and Jeanette had each other. Bruce had cricket but he couldn't focus on the game. A careless mistake for the top-order batsman. A lacklustre reaction to a bouncer ended in a nasty head injury. Bruce eventually lost everything to cricket. His friends and now his eyesight. The years piled on like runs on a cricket scorecard, but poor Bruce was stuck in the past like a batsman who never left the crease.

Dr. Marshall tapped on Bruce's shoulder. He had said enough.

'How about we stop here today,' said Dr. Marshall. 'Any plans for the weekend?'

'Plans? Oh, a must go country.'

'Are you attending a funeral?'

'A ongl funeral piiple go country fa?'

'I'm sorry, I just assumed people only leave the city for that sort of thing.'

'Iz a wedding. Ewan and Jeannette tying di knot and mi a di best man.'

'Congratulations!'

'Yo sound like a mi a get hitch.'

'No, but this is an opportunity to reconnect with people and have some human interactions.'

'Anything yo seh boss. Just don't look fi mi next week.'

'Mr. Parry, this wedding may be the answer you're searching for. Don't miss it.'

'Yo think so?'

'Breathing fresh air, recapturing the dazzling magic of your childhood can only be good.'

'Backside, dat a di best advice mi ever get from yo and iz a free advice to.'

'No, the best thing is this, remember to take a gift for the lovebirds.'

'Hmmm, a hav a great mind carry dat painting mi do a di old folks' home.'

'I didn't say that!'

Bruce walked out laughing, leaving his bat and ball behind. Dr. Marshall examined the bunka bat and the cricket ball, shook his head, and burst into a belly laugh.

The following day Bruce caught a country bus back home. It was an arduous drive, but he enjoyed every minute of it. Every bump in the road and each squeeze he had to endure was greeted with a smile across his face. The bus stopped for a few higglers to get off and through the window, he watched the cyan-blue sky blushed in ochre, vermilion, and magenta as sunray fingers caressed the horizon behind the hilltops. Two black girls draped in colourful madras dresses came walking up the dirt path with their sun-kissed skin, sparkling in the late evening sunlight. Neatly folded laundry balanced on their heads with the river water still soaked in the hem of their dresses and trickling down their charcoal calves—toned from all the walking and hefting to wash clothes at the waterhole. They flashed lightning-bright smiles at Bruce gazing at them as they shilly-shallied home. The country was truly magical, and Bruce relived the magic like a child. He saw his old house, his old school, and the stretch of road that fronted Jeanette's yard.

At the wedding, Bruce learned that Jeannette and Ewan were expecting, and they planned on naming the baby Leroy. The cuckoo finally brought an egg to the nest. Whole again, the gang of four. It made Bruce happy but he kept his fingers crossed that it would be a girl so Jeannette's big mouth could put her in trouble again. Ewan loved the painting Bruce gifted them, but it left Jeannette a little puzzled. It was a portrait of an upright cricket bat with two blue balls.

'A think wi should ask him why di ball dem blue,' Jeannette suggested.

'Yo sure? A don't want bother him spirit,' Ewan whispered.

'Di cricket balls puzzling unu no true?' Bruce asked.

'Well,' Jeannette and Ewan chimed.

'Wid Ewan tied to you, him ago laan di meaning a blue balls,' said Bruce.

Ewan and Bruce cackled in laughter, but Jeannette was still confused. Bruce hugged her and asked, 'Who a big head now?' Ewan called for the photographer to get a picture of them before Jeannette and Bruce removed their buried axes. The shutter clicked, whirred, and flashed and Bruce was back at his window. The weather had changed. Lightning crackled as dried leaves carried away in the wind. They hung like frayed threads—orts, unravelled from the sun's golden cotton spool. Another curtain twitched across the road. With one finger, Bruce closed the drapes and meandered through his memorabilia. His hands passed over the walls, counting the images he could not see. He paused at a faded newspaper clipping, which read:

HE DIDN'T SEE IT COMING! A BOUNCER ROBBED TEEN OF SIGHT SET ON CRICKET STARDOM.

Bruce Parry crawled back into the bed and curled in the foetal position. A moment later, an empty pill bottle fell out of his hand. It rolled until it stopped against a wall.

Then only silence remained in the room.

Death Comes in Threes

'Kevin, come here little bit.'

She was the kind of woman who'd wait until you were doing something before demanding your attention; the type to call you back to the yard when you'd already walked a mile. I went with the rake held up to my chest.

'Oh, you were raking?'

'Yes, Aunty.'

'Anyway, Pat just called me to the fence and pinch it tell mi that Piggy's body float up all the way in Ginger Bottom.'

I could feel a disappointment coming on.

'Just last week they chopped a goat thief to death in Labyrinth,' she said. 'Death comes in threes.'

There it was! I was waiting for it. Until death—whoever that was—killed a third person, I would be stuck in the yard catching the house colour. Then again, that blasted Piggy should count as two, since he was both a fool and an idiot. He got to go abroad and decided to take a last swim in Jamaica because he didn't think there were rivers where he was going. And who steals a goat this time of year? I thought that was a Christmas season thing. These two had to spoil it for me.

I hadn't heard Aunty come out. Usually, her hip would have shoved the mahogany dinner table, set halfway in the doorway. But she had gone and fretted away her weight. Now she and her clothes were in malice, the kind only seen between a shade and its lampstand. Pastor Parry, her husband, just up and left one day. Rumour had it that he had found foreign woman and was living somewhere on the north coast. Aunty was never the same. Her days were spent searching for what was left of her mind in Massa God's empty sky. And tormenting me.

'Yo mouth moving but yo not saying anything.'

'I'm not saying anything, Aunty.'

'Please to stay right in this yard, you hear mi?'

Not a backside. I had spent all summer collecting empty bottles, selling them fifty cent a piece to buy my goggles. You know how many people called me 'bakl police' for the extent to which I searched high and low for those bottles? All that sacrifice would be in vain. Not a backside.

It was August 1992. The guinep crop was coming to an end and the leaves that remained crisped-up and fell like it was nobody's business. Together with the whitish Ackee blossom brushed off by the bees before the daily rake the yard looked as if it had caught fire the night before. I sat in the crotch of the Parson Brown orange tree with my face skyward. It was then I thought about you. Yes, you in that iron bird being flown to some other interesting place. I wondered what us inland folks looked like to you from up there. Maybe nothing like resort beaches littered with sweet almonds and sea biscuits. I imagined your eyes must be those of a big, black John Crow. One caught up into the heavens on the warm morning air. Free, and with a good view of everything. I closed my eyes and pictured it all.

Hills humped and bowed towards the White River Valley—a herd of Jamaica Blacks drinking at a watering hole. Out from the rocks, the river oozed and silvered on the green the way snails ruin a callaloo crop. Houses cotched on the hillsides. Cookfires smoked as if coal kilns had broken too soon. The sky, a freshly washed blue sheet spread out on a line. Clean. Except for darker shades of blue in places like wet spots waiting on the sun. And the breeze was a screech, the likes of a mongoose chased by a culling mob. It came over the backs of each hill wrapped in a smell that was sweet, fresh, and rotten at the same time. But I didn't have those eyes. Hell, I couldn't even go past the orange tree let alone leave the yard. And I envied you. Yes, you in that iron bird going someplace interesting.

What I had was a fan broom, plastic and somewhat tooth-less; a dirty yard, and the raw sun waiting to ride on my neck back while I rake.

Markie and I had plans to go to the river. He was just recovering from a serious case of constipation, brought on by stuffing his gut with too many young guineps. He told me that his granny's remedy did the trick. Something to do with drinking lamp oil, a big common pin and laying across his granny's lap. Long story short, he was frequenting the outhouse again.

I'd known Markie since Basic School. He was one of the few people who knew that 'Kevin' wasn't my real name. Aunty wanted that name on my age paper, something she never got around to. We had everything in common, that Markie and me, except he was 'fourteen going on forty'—a manliness that caused trouble for both of us. Aunty never liked us being together but with only a hibiscus fence between the two houses, we were pretty much 'bench and batty'. That was how we came up with the grand idea to meet behind the big guango tree and make a dash for the river. The extra hands made the work lighter. Aunty didn't object. It was a perfect plan.

You probably asking yourself why I was so fixed on going to the river. Well, it was shrimp and bussu season and bussu caught a good price at the square, where soup kitchens stood in wait for the tourists in buses on their way to tubing at the old Spanish bridge in Endeavour.

I agreed to stay in the yard. Pawed the rake and scraped leaves left, right and centre. Then over the cackling of dried leaves came a call for breakfast. I only saw Aunty's frock tail wheel past the croton patch at the side of the house as she headed back to the fence. She and Vee occasionally shared dreams and had their talks—old maids are gluttons for gossip. At the top of their qualm list was how women from abroad were taking away the good men on the island. It always puzzled me how these two seers couldn't discern that their men were going to leave them. Especially Pat. The amount of big lick she got from Earle the end of their relationship should not have come as a surprise. Anyway, I got in the house before the puss and took a few of the fried dumplings in my pocket to eat while I worked. Ride and whistle, that's what old people call it when you don't have the luxury to sit and eat.

It was never going to be easy to slip Aunty's hawk eyes especially now that she was standing out in the open with a clear view of the guango tree. I prayed for something to call her back inside the house or even a mild stroke or heart attack to give me a window to slip away. Believe me, I didn't want her dead but sometimes I wished she would have left me alone. Slowly the fried dumpling crammed in my cheeks started tasting a little like rotten leaves, a little like blighted ackee blossoms and a lot like disappointment.

Markie stepped through the hedgerow. Two straw bags in hand, ready to haul leaves and head to the river.

'How many times I tell you not to walk through the fence?' Aunty barked.

'Is a slap him want. Him know better!' Pat chimed in.

'Hard of hearing! No blasted ears hole!'

'No ears hole,' Pat echoed.

'But it need the two of them to carry the little leaves?' Aunty hissed her teeth and kicked a few leaves near her feet.

'Look man, you hard-of-hearing Markie, carry the leaves and you Kevin, continue raking.'

She had both hands akimbo. Nose turned up until we could see the white of her eyes. And just like that, we were right back at square one. Markie left with the two bags on his shoulders. Whispered to me that he would be waiting but not for the entire day so I should try and meet him later. We exchanged bird calls, kept the plan alive but my wings were clipped. I didn't hear Markie after a while. At that point it didn't look as if I was going anywhere. Aunty and Vee stood under the shade of the aralia and hibiscus talking, while I roasted in the sun.

I was almost sunstruck when I heard a small voice: 'Hol' dog.' The voice was so low it sounded like a small child's. Down at the gate stood Pakool with a carton box on his head. An old farmer who had been frequenting the yard ever since Pastor Parry left. If I didn't know better, I would think he had taken a liking to Aunty. Our eyes made four. He held up his hand. I held up my hand. He didn't move. Coward. I dropped the rake and went and fetched this grown man. We met at the Parson Brown tree; he asked me to help him take down the load off his head.

'You want me to get Aunty?'

'She's here?' he asked in a whisper as if his voice was trapped at the back of his throat.

'She's talking to Pat.'

'Lawd, Pat mouth can't tame.'

'Okay Pakool. I have raking to do so you can wait on the verandah.'

'I'm alright where I am. I don't want Vee to know my business.'

He leaned on the orange tree. Knocked out his pipe on the side of his water boot. Grounded a leaf of dried tobacco in his palm and prepared his smoke.

'Yo not going to rake?'

'That is not what I want to do. I want to go to the river.'

'Aunty not having it?'

'How yo know?'

Pakool laughed and shook his head. A pearly white smog left his pipe.

'We are all rivers, you know?'

'Rivers?'

'Yes, rivers running in and out of each other until we end up in the sea.'

'I don't think Aunty is any river, more like a pond; she's never leaving this yard again.'

'No, she's a tree.'

'I still think she's a pond.'

'What if you're a tree and Aunty is a wall?'

'Man, how all these riddles going to help my situation?'

'I want to be a bird, so I can fly away!'

'Tell you what bird, let Aunty get this little parcel for me.'

'Yes, Pakool.'

'What are you? River or tree?'

Pakool said nothing. I didn't think he was that sensible. If Pakool didn't speak anyone would think he was a madman. He made me realize that we all had problems. And we all were looking for someone else to blame for them. He dusted his pipe and left.

Aunty dragged her slippers through the crabgrass on her way back to the front of the yard.

'Kevin?'

'Yes, Aunty.'

'Remember not to leave this yard.'

'Mass Pakool left something for you.'

'Who?'

'Pakool.'

'That old goat. You don't let him back in this yard without telling me.'

'Yes, Aunty.'

I had almost given up on the river when Pastor Parry drove up in a brand-new cherry-red station wagon Lada. Two years this man hadn't shown his face. But lo and behold, like a lamb to the slaughter, preacher man came home with a lady friend.

It was a big girl. I wasn't raised to make fun of anyone, but you couldn't tell them apart from a mouse on a dollar bread.

The rolls in her side gathered up all the fabric in her frock leaving nothing to the imagination. The worse part, she had on spike heels, so every step leaned to the side like a loaded market truck going through Fern Gully.

They had hardly stepped off the road when Aunty alighted from the verandah and started grabbing stones.

'But si mi dying trial today,' she said.

I kindly took myself out of harm's way. Pastor Parry, too. He went back to save the new car leaving his lady friend to face the stones alone. She skipped, hopped, and gambolled about like a moko jumbie midway a fall. This was the window I'd prayed for all morning. I couldn't tell you how the dus' up ended because by the time I heard the Lada tires peeling up the road, I was miles away. Perhaps death might just have got his third victim after all.

When I got to the square, everybody with anything to sell was there.

I headed downstream through a bushy lane, lined with hedgerows that were thickened by sweet wood trees and Black Wist. After battling a red poll that blocked the path, I almost got a heart attack when a speckled bantam flew across my face. I made it to the water. Gave out a bird cry. 'Cooh!' was the reply. Markie was there.

'Boxcover, yo mek it man!'

'Wouldn't miss it fi di world.'

'How yo escape?'

'Long story brejin, let's catch some bussu.'

'Okay boss man, this may be the last time I will see you alive caaz Aunty must kill yo later.'

After sinking the last calabash, Markie and I sat on a river stone eating leftover crab bait—mostly coconut and saltfish. We could hear them playing in the water upstream. All the girls had come to bathe at the same hour today.

We had to take a peek. On hands and knees, we crawled through the wild coco yams. Sunlight, pressed through the bamboo leaves, fell on the purple watergrass like rusty chicken wire. Soft, grey loam wriggled through our fingers and caked to our knees. It was soft and silent. But before we could get anywhere near the frolicking, the girls started screeching like crows in a swarm feed.

'Put one more foot forward and I wet you up with this panty-water,' one girl said, stooping to hide her nakedness. They started wheeling water from their undergarments.

'Don't mek the panty-water touch you,' Markie cried. 'It wi mek yo woklis!'

We took a hasty retreat, trailed by cries of 'rape!' and 'peeping Tom!'

Markie answered in fine style at a clear distance: 'Who waan rape any a you? After wi no like board. Unu tough laka board.'

'Tough like yo muma?' one girl fired back.

Markie wanted to throw stones, but I held his hand. We were in the wrong and we were outnumbered. As hard as it was to swallow being called a 'peeping Tom', it would be harder to live with being thrashed by a band of girls.

Markie asked if I had seen anything and began drawing a figure of a naked girl on a black river rock. He drew a big *bush* for the girl and joked how she was a dreadlock down there.

'Can't even piss straight but yo inna man and ooman bizniz.'

The man voice frightened us. We both looked around and there stood Mad Dwight, hands folded behind him, no black in his eyes and foaming at his mouth.

'A bet a kill unu today!' Mad Dwight showed his hands with a cutlass in each, sharpened white from the throat to the point.

He made a chop. The cutlass sang out as it got stuck in a low limb from a quickstick tree. Mad Dwight fought to free his cutlass. We galloped off the rock and headed back upstream at birds' speed.

The girls screamed out again as we approached the river: 'Wet dem up! Wet dem up!'

'Mad Dwight! Mad Dwight!' we bawled out to them.

Like frogs leaving the river, they all leapt to the banks, naked—not keen on hiding and we no longer interested in looking.

Nobody knew Mad Dwight was out of the madhouse. Nobody was out when Mad Dwight walked the streets. That double cutlass wielding madman would chop at even the breeze. He'd have no reservations chopping us.

So, we ran. When we came up on the cow pasture over-run in cow-itch, that didn't stop us; we ran through it. The common leading to the road had more Shame Old Lady than grass, still we didn't stop; we ran through all that prickle barefooted. The road was almost in sight when a girl fell. We turned to check on her, but there Mad Dwight was, attached to us like a shadow. We had to fling a few rocks to slow him enough for the girl to make it up to the road.

We ran up to the square. It looked nothing like when I had passed by on my way to the river. Fresh marl plugged the potholes and whitewash daubed on every living tree made it a spectacle in anticipation of the tourists. The row of shops sparkled in happy yellow at top and grey skirting to mask the dirt and marl. And like the shops, every face was made up to look pleasant to make the foreign money. Well pleasant until we came along. Ms. Mary, a kind shopkeeper, took the girls in. News of Mad Dwight put business on pause. Shutters came down on all shops. Ms. Mary's shop door had to be pushed up from the outside, so that was for Markie and me to do to save the women. Yes, those same women who wanted to make us worthless.

When Mad Dwight got to the square, we could only hide in the gutter under a culvert. He swooped down on us and started jamming the blades in the drain. We crawled to the other side and out of reach. He took a bamboo pole and started ramming the hole like he was invading a rat's nest. Markie got out on the other side first and reached back to pull me out. My right heel was burning like I stepped in Satan's chamber pot. It was sliced clean and hanging from a thin scab of flesh.

'Run Markie, a won't make it,' I called out.

'A not leaving you, him haffi kill di two a wi.'

I pulled through the rest of the culvert and slid down into the gutter where I was covered in some fat signal grass. I could see the road, but I was well camouflaged. Mad Dwight dropped the piece of bamboo and grabbed his machetes, dragged them on the road. Fire gashed and danced at him feet as the blades grumbled laka two mongrel dogs readying to attack each other. All the taste left my mouth. Markie froze stiff laka freshly steamed gabardine pants seam. Dwight wheeled the blades as if he was in a Kung Fu movie. He sliced through a banana tree a couple of times. It was no match for his machetes. The banana stem shattered as the overlapping leaf sheaths came apart laka dry-rot exercise book. He grinned and taunted some more, knocking off the heads from a few blades of guinea grass on his way towards Markie. By the time Dwight stepped into the gutter, a black hearse scratched tyres 'round the corner with two big speakers blasting Grace Thrillers' *Around God's Throne.* The driver pressed foot on the brake and steered the runaway vehicle so it faced back where it was coming from. Same time, a casket burst through the back door with a loud sound laka thunder and cartwheeled cross the road towards us. On the last tumble, a body—all dried up and looking laka suck-out bag juice—somersaulted and then spread itself in the middle of the road. The brute frightened. He dropped his weapons and jumped into the root of some ginger lilies at the roadside. The two men from the hearse sprang into action. They gathered up the cadaver barehanded, loaded the hearse and slammed the boot door shut.

All this time I was signalling Markie to come in the gutter and let us crawl 'way but him just stood there looking laka when cow lost the hinges on him mouth.

Luckily for us, as the hearse moved off, a patty van was creeping down the road. It had 'bout four people dressed in white coats with their heads out the windows. You could tell they were looking for something or someone. Their heads kept surveying the place in all directions the way thieves survey people's things during the day and come back night-time for it.

When Mad Dwight saw the patty van, him scratch-out from under the flowers and scaled up a big oilnut tree. He had forgotten about chopping anyone. The hunter became the hunted.

Markie found his voice again. 'See'm deh.'

'Weh him deh?' one of the white-coat people enquired.

Markie pointed to the treetop. Dwight tried to slip out and escape but two of the men alighted from the vehicle and swooped down under the tree. Dwight had to mount back to the top. He was stuck up there. They ordered him down, but he clung to the branches and behaved as if nobody could see him. The other two people parked the van and came out with syringes and a straitjacket in hand. Now it was obvious that they were from whatever madhouse Dwight escaped from.

People opened their shops and slowly started gathering back on the road to see them capture Mad Dwight. Markie came down to help me out of the gutter. He used a stone to beat the heel until the bleeding stopped, covered it in rotten banana trunk and tied it with his shirt. We then crawled back onto the road together and watched with the others as the health authority tried to catch their man.

'Look how him chop off this one foot,' one woman started to inform the crowd.

'I cut it on a rum bakl,' I tried telling her, but I guessed it wasn't as dramatic as being chopped by a madman because she kept repeating the same lie through the crowd. She poked the throng into a frenzy laka wasp's nest until they were a buzzing mob. They wanted blood. And she was leading them to it.

'Don't come any closer,' the lone woman of the four health workers begged.

'Let us deal with him our way,' the soup man started mouthing off with his ladle in his hand.

'Him a somebody pickney to,' Ms. Mary reminded them.

'Put him down like di dog he is,' the woman playing mob leader started shouting.

'Mi ready.' I mouthed the words to Markie, and he picked me up piggyback and we slipped through the crowd and headed home.

'Aunty must kill yo fi real this time,' Markie murmured with what sounded laka little fear in his voice, 'An' yo not even can run.'

I kept quiet and pondered the many ways I could get out of the thrashing that was waiting for me. I thought about getting back in the yard and pretending that I got cut down by the guango tree, but the news had travelled fast. Aunty was waiting for us on the verandah ready to dish out the backsiding. Markie dropped me at the bottom of the steps, pulled the shirt off my foot and bolted through the fence. He left me to face Aunty alone. I couldn't believe that he was more afraid of Aunty with a comb in her hand than Dwight with two machetes.

'Wah happ'n to you?' she barked, while she stepped over a pile of rocks she had gathered in the centre of the verandah and rushed towards me.

I could only lift the foot to show her. The banana bark fell off. The piece of foot bottom flapped over and revealed the round bone in the heel. Aunty grabbed her chest and went silent. The black of her eyes rolled back in her head and she started backing up. Her feet hit the rockpile, which sent her flying. She hit her head and didn't move. I hopped on the good foot to fetch the smelling salt. One whiff of it and she jolted back to life, but she still wasn't saying anything. I knelt over her and kept fanning with my hand and calling out to her:

'Aunty! Aunty! Aunty!' I shouted and the tears came running down my face. I called out to Pat, but the dog in the yard was making a ruckus and a big quarrel could be heard coming over the fence. After a while, Aunty wiped the tears that had fallen on her face and opened her eyes wide to look at me.

'Stay deh call, Aunty,' she whispered, 'A soon pam yo inna yo head,' She finished the line with a little gesture from the hand still gripping the comb.

I was so happy that she was still alive that I just hugged her. And pressed my face against her bony hand and laughed aloud. She was so embarrassed, but she wasn't going to let me get away with any of it. She gripped my shoulder. Pulled me close and said:

'Who laugh last, laugh best. Yo just wait till mi feel better.'

Patvita

How do you mourn a dead baby?

First, if you're anything laka me, you know not to believe ev'rything the big degree people have to say 'bout such things—you already know to find out from someone who had to bury a child. If not, begin by taking a taxi from Ochi to Gayle. Tell the driver that you want him to drop you off at Wilderness Resort, in New Pen. Understand that this is not on his route so it will cost extra money and cause the rest of the passengers to bad-mouth you. Don't pay them any mind. Just tell the driver you will pay in foreign money, and he will take care of the murmuring. When you get to Labyrinth, chances are you will see a barefoot ooman roaming up and down the road or sitting at the post office. Stop the car. Offer to buy everyone a drink. That is your entry to get close to har. Depending on who gives you har name, she could be Patvita laka har pa, Vita, Pat, or Vee. I know har as Pat. She has first-hand experience 'bout mourning the death of a child.

Pat is Indian but she's not like the Punjabis selling jewellery at the Taj Mahal Shopping Center. She has a dark complexion laka har pa who use to sell coal. Her romp bounces laka bad cheques on ship days in Ochi and she has no taste for Indian men. Careful how you approach har though. You're technically still a stranger to the place and she don't like people looking at har long. You see, Pat was my neighbour in Cascade and while she was pregnant, she and har husband Earle had a big fight. She lost the baby and Earle lost a big toe. Pat took it hard. She walked all hours a night laka warner ooman, crying for that child. She couldn't continue working as a schoolteacher and on top of it all, Earle find foreign ooman and move-out. That put a heavy burden on har mind laka hanging drapes on curtain rods. Har consciousness was barely holding up—things were too weighty on her head. Plus, when the man you love walk out on you, ev'ry barfly and fly-by-night think you're fair game.

'Yo don't want a man, Vee?' some teased, offering up each other when she walked by the bar.

'Mad gyal pudd'n gummy and nice but yo boun' fi lose yo knife cutting dat,' others mocked.

But deep down if Pat wasn't a fighter, they would jump at the chance to bed har.

'Man, I tell you, they are nothing but walking contradictions,' Pat would say at the top of her voice. 'They would kill you at the mention of eating ooman front but have so many delicious names for it: saltfish, pork, fishy and bake-bake like toto and pudding.'

You can tell this put har life in danger. She had to fight some more and so har pa came and took har back home. This didn't stop her fighting though.

She had a spiteful brother watching har laka hawk. Buzzer was a lazy, tampee-smoking ooman beater with the boniest chest you ever see. It's as if Maasa God stood behind his lump of clay and scraped His fingernails from front to back to form that ribcage. Buzzer wasn't always this way. He was a big mechanic on the Northcoast. Talented but love him liquor and smoke grass laka it going out of style. I don't remember which international event was happening in Jamaica at the time but they scooped up all the homeless people from off the roadsides so tourists wouldn't see them. Buzzer, drunk and sleeping on the road after payday, got swept up too and woke up in the Freeport lockup in Mobay. It was hell to get him out because of the way the young man carried himself. From then him hate the world and give up on life. At the least of things, you see him coming with him shoulders up under him ears laka smaddy midway a sneeze. Him always want to fight. I guess it was a way to reclaim the power they took from him when they locked him up. Him behave as if him was set over Pat, a wrong move that send him back to him maker early.

When their father died, Pat being the elder one, end up owning har pa possessions. Simply because Patvita left no will. The coal kilns, the land and the cows belonged to Pat and not Buzzer. People in the community sing this song when they see Buzzer coming:

'Mi pa dead an' gaan an' him no lef' no will him ongle lef' wan cow a fi di ole a wi. But mi bigga bredda him tek I weh from wi. Glory be to God; glory be to God a fi di ole a wi.'

This caused tension between the two. Things boiled over one day when a ripe kin man visit the yard. When the man left, Buzzer presented himself, stink of kaya smoke and rum.

'Yo tititit-tink no man a lili-live inna mi pa house?' he said, walking up to the verandah with a stone in one hand and a machete in the other.

Pat pretended not to hear him.

'A wiwiwiwi-wi bobobo-bon it flat, flat!' Buzzer slurred again.

'Go bon in hell man-to! Go find ooman and stop watching mi frock tail,' Pat answered.

Those words ignited a fire inside Buzzer. He ran up to the verandah mad laka him drink mad puss piss. As him set foot on the step, Pat held on to a rafter and give him one rahtid kick inna him chest. The blow sent him rolling off the hillside. Him pick up himself and started flinging some big stones at the house. One bounced off a column and hit Pat in har head-side and she fell. She stayed still and play laka she dead. When the coward didn't see har move, he grabbed a piece of cow rope and headed for the woodland. Buzzer chose to string himself up on an Ackee tree than be mobbed by the community. After that, no man don't test Pat. Some called her obeah ooman and even though people think the high colour man don't really love har they never utter it for Pat to hear. If you ask har about har relationship, she will tell you that country people a kunu munu. Meaning that them stupid.

It's not like Pat eating out of the garbage or stripping naked for John Public. You and I know that mental health don't manifest the same way in everyone. It's not like there's a yardstick to measure who is sane or not. Truth is, we're all as different as mango price in the same market.

Now when you approach har, don't mince words or patronize har. She still has her wits about har. She still demands a glass of water and says, 'Don't spit in it,' laka she talking to her schoolchildren. The barkeep might not want to serve har but flash the foreign money and make sure they oblige har. Allow har to cross her legs at the ankles and get comfortable. And if she picks up a wild fowl, opens the beak and spits in its mouth then massages the craw while talking to the bird laka 'nother person, you should relax. Treat it as normal something. She will trust you. Walk with har on the road. Scream 'green bush' when a mongoose cross before you. Pat like it when har company know the culture. Don't force har to tell you anything. Wait on her. When she's good and ready you will hear everything. When she tells you that walking barefoot keeps har close to har baby in the ground, you're not supposed to laugh. Take off your shoes in solidarity. Listen to everything and repeat laka you making a shopping list.

'Stay away from school gate so people carrying and collecting dem pickney don't make you sad.'

'Don't tell anyone di name yo had fi yo child so dem can use it.'

'Kip di same bath set and hand it down to any other child yo have.'

'Get a fren to tell yo it wasn't your fault. One who know 'bout Ol' Hige and how it come fi yo baby.'

'If yo don't waan bring another child into the world, drink pear leaf and dog blood bush.'

Don't repeat that! Tell har you must leave immediately but you will come back to eat fish with har at Wilderness Resort. You won't go back. When you walk back to the post office, do it at bird's speed. If she follows you, stop and standstill laka bush. She will go by you laka two strangers. After a week or so, go back through all Pat told you and make sense of it. You will see the length a woman is willing to go to be close to her child even in death. Understand that a woman will have to live with the absence of that child for as long as she lives and everything, even what should have been will remind her of the loss. Remember that the dog blood bush recommendation was never an instruction but said in a way for you to make your own decision because only a woman should decide on how to deal with such a thing as losing a child.

Only a woman should decide how to heal.

Spana and Country

'Blood! Blood! Blood and fire!' The screams cracked and splintered through the darkness laka pimento wood under bolo-man axe.

'Black flag and chapaalin!' The voice continued wailing from Jeffrey Town, coming towards Coffee Walk. The mongrel dogs perk up laka good watchdogs. And so howling dogs and this ooman voice carried on as if it was a game of call and answer.

Spana jumped up. She looked around the room.

'Who yu?' she shouted. 'Good ting mi heart not weak.' A duppy bat flew off the wall and pitched on the ceiling

'Come out ya nastiness!' Spana argued with the moth. 'Don't carry yo dead bizniz ya soh!'

Her dog, Cool Ice, scratched out from under the cellar and bounded through the banana walk.

'Come Cool Ice!' Spana called out. 'Mi don't know weh Country find this coward dog. Cool Ice! Cool Ice! Cho backside!'

'Death a come a Coffee Walk! Blood a go run! Head a go ruol! Wiipin and muonin, laad. Fish and bred! Fish and bred!' the warner ooman bawled out again. This time like she was at the entrance of the parochial road Spana lived on.

'Weh she a go wid so much noise dis early hours a di mawning?' Spana moaned.

She got up and moved towards the dresser.

'Ev'ry one mos go someday,' Spana said flashing out the fire from a matchstick she used to light a candle.

'Ban unu beli an' baal! Set unu hous' in aada! No obeah man can help unu, no 'mounta gyaad ring kyan siev yo!' cried the ooman.

Spana knocked her chest and belched. 'All mi can go anytime now,' she moaned again.

Markie, sleeping in the other room, could hear her. It was normal occurrence, just as day came after night. He listened for Spana's belch to follow. The big belch was his cue to get up and set on the tea. He started living with Spana ever since he was placed on the chopping blocks at his hotel work. He had to move out of the rented house in Old Buckfield. There was no chance for him to move back into his mother's house in Cascade because he gave her a proper cussing-out when he got the job and his own place. After seeing all that light on the Northcoast, the countryside was a backward step for Markie. It meant losing the parties, the girls and the social life that defined him. It was the fastest you ever see a young man quail up and give up on living.

Markie quickly grated the green kola nuts and wait for the powder to turn red before putting it to boil.

'Mek sure di bizzy red before yo put it inna di pot,' Spana warned.

Markie didn't answer. He was used to his nana treating him laka lili bwai despite being only a couple of months short of his fortieth. He picked up the cheese pan and headed out to the common to get cow's milk from Mass Bertie. Not something Markie liked doing because, for the little milk, he had to help water the cows, carry grass, or listen to Bertie go on and on about farm work in Connecticut, 'Laad God,' he thought. Still, it was better than Spana carrying on 'bout drinking black tea.

The warner ooman cleared Bedstone and was heading for Rose Street with her travelling circus of barking dogs. The morning took its own little time to ripe. Markie returned to find the yard filled with people chatting. Cool Ice was coming up out of the banana walk with a wagging tail. The poor dog decided to return just as Spana was emptying her chamber pot. Splash! Cool Ice, covered in sputum and piss, darted back through the banana walk.

'Cool Ice, sorry darling!' Spana cried out.

'Spana!' Country called out.

'Hooo,' Spana answered.

Country had his transistor radio pressed on the side of his head. 'Di man dem a lif di curfew tideh,' he said.

'Backside, dat mean market a kip?'

'Wait noh man, di announcement noh mek yet!'

'Weh yaa seh, Country?' Miss Gwen enquired.

'Something 'bout Maas Kirlew!' Hap said.

'Mi seh notn 'bout Kirlew man? A soh deaf iez gi laiad problem. Curfew mi seh man!' Country barked.

'Weh yo seh, curfew a free up?' Gretel asked while knocking out an empty lotion bottle in his palm.

'Mek di man taak no man. Mi kyaan haadly hie mi iez wid yo a pam-pam dat deh empty bakl inna yo han migl!' Spana bellowed.

The yard went quiet. Country kept nodding his head as if the Prime Minister was talking directly to him. Everyone else wouldn't even breathe too hard as they waited. Markie pushed up the firewood and poured the cow's milk into the pot. Country flashed his Bruce Golding cap off his head and slapped it on his leg. He almost hit the pot off the fire.

'Wah di man seh?'

'Spana, market a kip! Di curfew lif'!' Country announced to the glee of everyone.

'Look at God! Mi did a worry seh di yam would spoil,' said Hap.

'Gretel come cut two plant'n fi mi,' said Miss Gwen.

'Beg Dracula fi do it fi yo.'

Dracula had appeared out of nowhere and fit himself neatly in the group.

'Somebody crying blue murder when yo si him,' said Spana pointing her mouth at Dracula.

'See thee say nothing,' Dracula warned.

'Gweh from ya soh criminal!' Spana fired back.

Dracula was known to soak his fingers in vinegar until they were slim as thread. That way he could easily slip them in people's pockets. Everybody got busy gathering loads for the Wednesday market at Coronation. Nobody noticed that Dracula had disappeared until Country couldn't find the radio.

By midday, the market loads were stacked on the roadside. Market had seemed a sure bet until then but there was no driver for the market truck. Kirk, the truck driver, was hospitalized with the Coronavirus. But his ooman wanted to go to the market as well so once there was a driver nothing was stopping them.

'Wah 'bout Rennie,' Spana asked.

'Rennie dead from last year,' Country replied.

'A lie!'

'Wi no charter bus go all a funeral down a Chapleton.'

'So, a Clarendon Rennie come from? Mi nay know! Bwai, mi hope say a straight under di orange tree side a papa and mama mi bury,' said Spana pointing at the graves under the navel fruit orange tree.

'Right down a Pimento Walk yo going side'n yo husband,' Country remarked.

'Cat drive truck noh true?' Gretel asked, not to anyone specific, more like searching through his mind to try and remember.

'Markie, run go over Cat yaad and si if him wi carry wi go town,' said Spana.

'Man, how yo fi sen out di big man laka bwai-bwai so?' Country scolded Spana.

'Don't try come between mi and mi grandson. Yo waan go market or noh bada ask di man?

'Cat will carry wi,' said Markie as he served Spana a cup of tea.

'How yo know dat?' Country questioned him.

'Cat noh have noh money right now, so if him kyan mek a dollar him not refusing it.'

'A true, mi hear seh gunman hold him up inna Lee bar last week,' said Hap followed by a gut laugh.

'A noh so mi hear it. Mi hear seh gunman walk in pon dem holding dem cock!' Miss Gwen fought to say between bursts of laughter.

'Dem cock?' Gretel asked.

'Rooster, Gretel. Weh yo noh check yo iez dem? Lee do cock fight baka di bar,' said Country. 'Not wah yaa tinkin 'bout.'

'Ask di man yaa Markie,' Spana said again.

Markie left to go and get Cat. The gunman story was no joke. 'Di gunman never jus rob Cat and him friends but dem get some licks drop inna dem skin as well,' Markie wanted to say but then he would have to explain how him know those details. He couldn't let Spana know he was there and narrowly escaped the flogging. He remembered how the gunman ordered the men to pile onto each other's backs and threatened to set them ablaze. 'No fire in here tonight sir,' he remembered Cat hollering. It made him giggle to himself.

Cat and Markie returned and announced for the crew to get themselves ready. Cat took the truck to Pumphole to get gas. He noticed an oil leak underneath the old Bedford and got it patched up in some sort of way. Then he picked up marketgoers along the way back for the Coffee Walk massive. Soon after, the truck was buried under a mountain of wooden boxes and crocus bags, which caused it to creep slowly laka snail. It carried dasheen, banana, pumpkin, and coconut. An oil slick—laka slime trail—tailed behind it all the way back to where it was last broken down. The old Bedford lumbered through the verdant hills of Saint Catherine until it was tagging alongside the foaming Río Cobre that galloped below the road in a well-watered valley. Redwood trees left naked from the Easter breeze were like scattered burnt wood in a cold fireplace against the ashy sky. Cat shifted the gearbox into low gear, the black truck shell trembled the way a food pot would midway through a boil. The scene was completed with the steady bubble and froth of the river over the peeping rocks. It was peaceful. Too peaceful.

Journey-wearied higglers, crammed in with the loads like livestock, were flanked by bulky sidemen responsible for the hefting to load and offload everything. Two old women in the front seat began arguing over space, 'Yo can eat less yo know' the one up against the window said.

'At least mi not using mi teeth to dig mi grave laka you,' the other one snapped while tapping on her mouth.

Together with Cat 'round the steering wheel, they completed the band of pariahs, bringing the market to town. The only trouble, they were travelling blindly into the Bog Walk Gorge. There could be an accident, it could rain, and the road flood. There was no phone reception in the gorge and with Country's radio gone and none in the truck, they had no way of finding anything out.

A few minutes later, as the shy evening sun sheltered its smile behind the mountains, the crunch of the tires over the stony road got lost under the quarrel of the two women. Cat turned to quiet them and, at that moment, came upon an object in the middle of a corner. Tires screeched, the horn blared, and everyone cried out to the heavens as the truck careened off the road.

As they fell, their whole life flashed before their eyes. The tender reeds that banked the untamed Río Cobre buckled under the weight of higglers, bananas, and coconuts thrown from the truck. Three women were sitting atop the market boxes when the ride started to flicker, light and dark laka firefly behind. It was a mad race as people and produce barreled down the ravine. They banged, crashed, bounced, and fell on their way to the throat of the river. A green lime for protection escaped one woman's bosom, a few copper cents scattered from another's apron while one woman lost grip on her pumpkin knife, which then got stuck in a wooden box. The evening sun glinted on the blade in every flip the old truck made.

The wheel of time started rolling backwards in flashes of rapid scenes from the past. A father had picked some limes for his daughter, and he gave her one to keep on her person. A stone's throw away, a woman and her husband stacked bananas together as sunlight pelted the shadows cowering beside them and a mother helped her young son with a banana trash katta to cushion his head from the load of pumpkins he carried. They're all waiting on the same Bedford truck going to the Wednesday market. Memories jerked about in every tumble as the women pondered life as a daughter, a mother, and a wife. Then everything stopped. Everything. Except high above the rolling slopes carved by a young river tumbling off the blue hills, lay a lazy Red Poll in the middle of the road with a skid mark skirted close to its hind leg. A lazy Red Poll, still chewing its cud.

Only Spana and the Río Cobre made it to the Kingston harbour. She floated as one drowned, atop a bag of pumpkins. She was up with the sun early Wednesday morning to catch the first sale. Coronation Market buzzed and shrieked laka honeybee swarm poked out of its sleep as vendors and shoppers bargained in the streets. Spana stood sweating like a river in the raw sun with her ears splitting from the banters between harried housewives and annoyed vendors. She caught no sale. She just stood there dripping in sweat. Such a funny thing. The more she wiped her forehead the wetter it became. She had no idea that she was in the hospital trying to wipe her tears with the hand she lost in the accident, while two figures done up in papier mâché lay motionless on either side of her.

Noontide disappeared. Shadows stretched twice the traffic on either side of the road as working folks double-stride home. It spread across the dilapidated buildings on Darling Street and dipped into the drains where those without toilets wheel their business in black scandal bags. The city soaked up that late evening amber glow. The last slice of sunlight dragged behind the sinking sun. Dragged laka brass anchor through the marsh, on the sand, then into the deep dark blue soul. Silence marked the death of the day. All left living turned their attention to the dark woman carrying that bastard child. She'll search high and low. She'll call out into the blackness for a man or two. Then morning will hear about some poor fools who didn't make it through the night.

Spana, Country and Markie will have people turning up their beds on a wall. Black flags and tarpaulin will be put up and people from far and wide will travel to Pimento Walk to eat fish and bread, witness the final rites, and throw dirt on their caskets.

Bull Buck and Duppy Conqueror

Hallo man. Don't pay loggerhead Buru any mind. I can see dat yo really want answers as to why not a grain of pimento is in Pimento Walk. Buru not able to help yo with dat. Ordering chicken back by calling out for chicken and knockin' his back is as good as his mind can ever be. Nobody else 'roun dis shop piazza old enough to answer such a question. But a can give yo one better. Yo ever ask yo'self why Ocho Rios not eight rivers? Bear wid me. Yo have White River, Cave River, Roaring River, and Turtle River. Dat not only four? Well maybe what is key to the answer yo seek is the fifth river called Fern Gully River. Don't ask mi 'bout the other three cause nobody still don't know them. By the way, not all folks come wid the stomach for some stories but a story like dis need not stomach but heart. Yo have the heart for it?

Me, Pakool, born and grow right here in Pimento Walk. And I'm as old as every tale 'bout this place. All the houses were built on a one-room plan—kitchen and outhouse dashed asunder. Poor folks didn't mind small dwellings. Their hearts and soul poured into the kitchen gardens that fronted the homesteads and the ten and two chil'ren dat sprung up like weeds in the yards. Back then, chil'ren were a poor man's treasure. The more the merrier. But not Bull's cottage. It was an unkind old cabin, with plenty baby clothes but no babies for a very long time. Loose floorboards, blood-rusted nails and rickety furniture told tales of a battered woman in a house where almost every baby died in the belly. Rose made it out alive, but the bitter house was not done killing babies.

When night come, everybody in the same family cooped-up in their own likl four walls. Chil'ren sometimes laid awake listening or watching their folks as they rustled under the covers and in two crop seasons, another snot-nose stranger appear 'roun the house. Rose too must have heard her ma and pa crackling like dry banana leaves in their shack because from time to time she had the neighbour's half-blind boy, Job, getting up to the same grown folks' deeds under the big mango tree. Dat was sure to be Rose's doing caus' Job was blind laka bat and with all the whippings he got for being hard of hearing, he had no ears to listen to his folks doing anything at nights.

Job was what you would call an imbecile. A grown man with the mind of a child; a rolling baby, who hit the ground hard a couple times. As a boy, he went out to set a springe to catch a bird, but the cruel guava branch trap flew early and almost blinded him in both eyes. Job's ailments made him no good for the fields, but he found work at Bull's slaughterhouse. An apprentice of sorts who prefer playing ride-the-donkey with the younger children in the grassy pastures than lifting dead animals and washing cleavers at the meat shop. Simply put, Job's big head gathered water. A mandora coconut, which made it easy to convince him.

Hol' on man. The story is a likl bit long but a soon get to the good part. Where was I? Ah yes, Job and Rose decided to rooks each other under the big mango tree. Two young, green mangoes swinging together. Not even the hot summer breeze could pass through them as it bowed the parched Guinea grass. Neither of the two had been kissed enough by sunshine to taste any sweet from their meeting. Leaned 'gainst the mango tree and still in clothes, the two shuffled like common fowls at a banana root. A pair of good eyes kept watch, but in the wrong direction. Bull came up the old path. He watched the two with jaw-tightening hatred. Rose reminded him of her mother who took the wings of the morning five crop seasons to dat day. People had it to say dat Beryl ran off with another man. Some claimed she jumped in Fern Gully River because of the drunkin beatings she got from Bull. And massa, he was drunk every night. Bull gave Job an almighty slap 'cross his back with his cleaver, sinking the shirt deep into his skin. Job dashed 'cross the cow pasture plucking on his shirt, deh try remove the slap. Rose quailed up at the sight of her pa. But Bull said not a single word, he jes turned and head back into town.

Dat night Bull came crawling on all fours. A grand show for the neighbours as he form say him drunk. Rose couldn't tell the difference. She was sound asleep, curved like a peg of orange. Moonshine peeped through the uneven wood slabs. Soon a terrible shadow was cast under the window where she slept. And Bull was a man to fear yo see. He was all muscles. Mi mean say, if yo fried the man for days yo still couldn't get even big gill worth a grease. Rose could not run. Bull did an unspeakable thing that night. Above the struggle, on the windowsill, a moth was caught in the web of a house spider. Its wings buzzed to a halt as the spider sucked it dry. It funny that when things laka this happ'n, the spirit too shame to stay in the body. Nothing more than she saw the whole thing as the moth and spider.

Rusty ceiling dust rained down as the old house shook. Bull cared not for Rose and her screams. He didn't have to. To village folks, wailing chil'ren at any hour meant a deserved thrashing. The rattling and dust-rain stopped. Only a dangling wing on a strand of web moved. Dead silence. The moonlight crept back into the room as Bull got up and left. Rose lay sprawled. A ripe pear splattered on a rock. She was still, face buried in the musty rags. The pickney suffered for days. Her head had gathered water, too. Her eyes leaked bitter tears. A wildfire burned between her legs. Sitting stung just as river water would, in the white-fleshed scrapes after running through Old Woman Razor grass.

Then massa, she started feeling bad laka how yo feel when it's mango season. People said she was hawking and spitting roun', roun' the place. Yo know dat sickness yo get from eating too many wormy mangoes? Yes, same so. One crop season later a baby fell out of her belly on the outhouse floor. It didn't cry. Stillborn them call it. What a heavy burden the pickney had to bear. She gathered up the thing from off the floor and swoops headlong in the pit latrine.

Now if Bull's secret at the bottom of his latrine was to ever come to light, it would have landed him in the wo'k house. It look laka say Job had seen something because he started behaving funny, funny. Not going to the meat shop and deh mouse, mouse 'roun the pit latrine. Bull wasn't taking any chances, so he cooked up a story how poor Job was tryin' to steal his cow. And cow thief need not go before the court in these parts when farmers have plenty good rope. What happen was dat it all played out in a grand hanging on the same big mango tree. A molasses-thick swarm of black folks gathered 'roun a battered black body, lidless and peering eyes dat don't see, bleeding into the banyan cord's sunken-kiss.

Look ya man! Bull swear blind that him get away with all of it. Bwai a tell yo when man wicked them really wicked. But ev'ry man have him time. Under a blood moon one night judgement and Bull crossed path. Drunk, he stumbled through the dark on his way home. Stink of rum and the slaughter-house, Bull buck up into a long-horned cow there in the dark. The beast went mad. Tail curled onto its back, head dipped and hooves stomping the dusty road. Butcher and beast faced off, but a cleaver was no match for an untied cow with two long horns. Bull only managed to lumber for a few cabbage patches when cane rum buckled his knees and pitched him flat on his face. The cow rammed its horns through flesh and dirt. A horn broke off and pegged Bull down. Pain latched his tongue between his teeth. He was never able to bawl out for help. The cow mortar him down a dutty and dragged him all the way over into some barbwire fence. The body was found next mawning with a horn through the heart and full of hoof marks laka dry mud at a cattle crossing.

Deep down, people in Pimento Walk knew Bull was a cruel man and dat it was only a matter of time before something terrible would come to him. But even worse, it was really fishy dat Bull pass on at a cow pasture where no cow was kept. The whole thing was a sign. Ev'ry man stop walk a night. It was no secret dat when a butcher man dead, yo could look out for plenty more dead to follow.

As yo know, before every burial, the dead is usually prepared for the great beyond in nine days. Nine days of singing, dancing, eating and grave digging. Bull's body needed to go by day three. The stink was causing folks to pinch their nose. Anyway, yo start to look a bit antsy. Mek a talk a likl faster.

Two days after Bull met his death, there was talks of burning the body and not burying it. But in the end, many people gathered at the old cemetery, not for the man but for the *mannish water*. Under a withering poui tree, a grave spot was found. Women from the Pocomania faith came too. They stood close to the graveside, where two hardy men whistled and stabbed at the mossy old mud. Their salty sweat-covered backs stank of old graves and rotten leaves. The women paced the dig with old spirituals, only pausing the Sankey hymns to chomp down on smoke-cured fish and fried cassava. The sharp lemony scent from the gravediggers' sugar and water cut through the funky fish smell. Dassa, a heavyset woman called out to the men not to waste the lime guts. And went back to preparing meat for the mannish water. Just a stone-throw away from the graveside, her little makeshift kitchen stood. She laboured over the meal hacking away at some roasted goat head, passing the meat through the lime-gut water, then plopping them in the pot to boil the soup. The little wattle-and-daub hut had flinty flavours of onion and goat meat puffing through ev'ry crevice. Goat head and roasted spices mingled, latched onto the brisk mawning air, and swirled laka one mad wind in a burning canefield.

Some coffin-dodgers followed their nose to the burial ground. They staggered and buzzed in circles laka one swarm of fruit flies drunk off cane liquor. There was a briny hint of herring and old tobacco dat shouldered with them. A meagre dog covered in mange and a snuffy cellar-scent drew close to the pot as well. Now each stir of the soup teased the air in peppery spices blended with traces of ram goat piss. It is not mannish water if it is not a man goat.

Dassa knelt to blow back life into the dying woodfire. Then through the rising smoke she looked. The dusty dog scent must have outwrestled the smoking pimento bark for the mongrel was almost on top of her. Dassa cuss two bad wud! They clap hard from her mouth laka gravel under a donkey's hoof running away from a padded hamper basket. Maybe the dog was deaf because it never even budge. She reached for the meaty wash water and doused the dog. Massa, the dog gathered its legs and bolted through the throng of singers. Pandemonium! The revivalists got in mire. Fish, cassava, and lemonade was all over the place. The bangarang pickled the air in wet dog and raw meat. It was now an angry mob. A defenceless dog. Would-be murder. But the 'twig of a dog' burrowed its way into an old grave where nobody could follow it. They only had a trail of foul odour, as if it was caught on a ribbon and blowing in the wind.

The little excitement didn't stop the crowd of people from enjoying Dassa's mannish water. Drooling mouths slurped and running nose dragged as soon as the goat head soup came off the boil. And by the time Dassa scraped the bottom of the pot, the crowd was no more than a handful of people.

Chamu, chamu ye tu-talk some, leave some.

Fear had fallen on Pimento Walk, so a message was sent to Scott's Hall to the Kromanti-speaking maroons to perform a ritual to ward off Bull's evil spirit. And in the dead of night, before the burial, goatskin drums and abeng thundered 'roun Bull's house. The village did not sleep dat night. Wails and ritual chants bellowed from the gut of the Tete man, leader of the maroon drummers. The spiritual ceremony carried on way into the morning when the Tete man got possessed by the ancestral spirits. The maroon leader stood up stiff and spoke: 'Chamu, chamu ye tu, a will talk some and leave some. Bird don't fly and him pickney walk. Bull pa rape him ma and dead in a wo'k house for di act. Bull did di same and two babies sleep at the bottom of the pit. One don't even have a name.'

Tete man collapsed. Mouths gaped wide and heads shook from side to side as the villagers listened to the revelation in disbelief. But before the cock crowed and under the last cover of night, the drummers took a silent march back into the mountains. The people remained antsy even though death itself had died and fear was about to be buried.

Daylight cut laka one machete slicing through sugarcane. Darkness fell. Bled. Covered in golden sap. The sun was a madman, wild and merciless. Sharp rays hurried across Pimento Walk, hacking at the shadows, bursting orange through the gloom laka open coal kiln. Wails of waking crows travel over ev'ry hilltop. Night either took flight or laid waste in the valleys. Bamboo, willow and guango trees all stretched out their arms and yawned as the mawning heat prized away night's cold fingers. Pupa Jeezus, massa, only hell fire hot laka dat mawning. It was a massacre. Sunlight walked through the headstones of the old church cemetery, stopping only to rest awhile 'gainst one old cedar door. Slant. Chopping it in half.

Back at the dead yard, while tongues wagged 'bout the Tete man's revelation, an old warner woman name Adlyn came to dress the body. She had a limp and a deep whooping cough. A trail of thick smoke escaped her nostrils as she puffed on a big cigar with the lit side in her mouth. People put up a likl fuss to stop her from dressing Bull, but nobody really wanted to cross her. Massa, Adlyn was a necromancer and obeah woman. One man bawled out 'Bull is dead. Nobody here gives a rat's behind, and neither should you.'

'Well, maybe the pimento should. It could be drying in the sun on that same twelve-foot-long galvanized zinc covering Bull's stinking corpse,' a woman in the crowd whispered.

Adlyn never even looked at any of them. She rolled Bull on a mahogany slab. The rotten flesh left on the zinc nearby carried the smell laka salted mackerel or corned pork barrel, cracked open for the first time. Jeyes Fluid and bloody water seeped between Adlyn's fingers. She stuffed the leaky holes with cotton and daubed what was left of Bull in ashes and rum-soaked pimento to mask the stink. A piece of stiff beige calico wrapped the body before it was laid on a bed of sawdust inside a government-issued pine box. Adlyn only removed her cigar once to make an utterance in her strange tongue. She spat red rum over the pine box. With her bare hands, she wrung the head off a chicken and sprinkled the hot blood on the dead body. Her ritual continued with parchment paper and thirteen rusty four-inch nails. She hammered the nails in the calico while saying to the dead body 'Four-inch nails now keep you in your new bed.'

She warned that the body should be in the ground by nightfall and all women who had relations with Bull must wear red undergarments for another six days so that Bull's spirit wouldn't fool with them in their sleep. Massa, a whole heap a man and them woman mash up cause of that very thing. But that is a story for another day.

By midday, people poured into the church from pulpit to pews. It was a long and dreary service. Ev'ry Jack man and woman had a memory to share. But Bull could not be kept above his grave much longer. Raw sun sitting atop of the church caused ashes and pimento to surrender to the stench. Church turn into one big funky scent. People got uneasy but Parson Brown harked and gagged on his sermon as if he was moving phlegm from his throat. He wouldn't have stopped preaching if they didn't strong-arm him midway his badmouthing the dead.

Church people headed straight for the dying poui tree. Nobody wanted to be caught downwind with Bull's casket leading them. It was a strange march to the graveside, everybody bolted for Bull's final resting place. In the fray someone bounced Dassa and sent her crashing onto the pine box. The body shifted. Few nails loosened. Bull's body rocked side to side in a sort of parched coffee beans between mortar and stick manner. All that didn't matter now because night was bounding over the hills and heading straight for town. Pallbearers took their feet in their hands and hurried for the hole prepared to mould up the dead. No final rites said at the graveside. Just a box-chuck into the hole and a mad scatter of dirt piled onto the pine wood.

No grave can hold my body down.

Nobody dared raising dat Sankey over Bull's body.

They wanted him to stay underground. They even dropped a big rock on the grave. Something still was wrong. Adlyn felt it. She was halfway home when the wind came howling laka one battered dog on a full moon night. Only there was no moon. Jes some lazy lightning trembling 'roun dark clouds. And they

113

hobbled laka spayed mongrels, tail-tucked and useless during heat. Fog crawled between ev'ry pimento tree, wrapping from the roots to the height of a man. Night and fog, laka cow caul, curled roun Pimento Walk. Picture a black racer and a yellow boa latched onto the same sleeping toad. House lamps and peenie wallies had no shine. Pimento Walk died a black death. Danger was in the wind lurking. Adlyn lit her cigar and started back towards Pimento Walk.

When Adlyn reached where Bull was killed, something cornered her in the darkness. Sounds of a jangling chain snaking over the sharp stones trailed the warner woman. She spun 'roun and paced slowly backwards, to confuse whatever was out there in the blackness.

'Ha! Brute, you know not whether a coming or going, show yourself.'

Well, most country folks understood never to front a bull or go behind a donkey, so Adlyn waited. A snort from the gloom roasted the night air. Beads of sweat walked down Adlyn's face, hot laka Satan's toenails. She crushed a green lime between her teeth and wheeled 'roun in maypole fashion.

'Come out if you bad,' she taunted.

And massa, two flaming eyes did come out to her. It was a big cow-like beast, dripping in blood and covered in thorny chains dat cut through its flesh. Adlyn was face-to-face with a rolling calf. She dug a line in the dirt with her heel, flashed her frock tail behind her and grabbed a lace-bark whip that was strapped on her leg. Crack! The split tongue whip kissed the waiting air, stopping the rolling calf. Adlyn circled the beast looking deep into those flaming eyes. Her fierceness drove some fear into the haunt. She hauled a bottle of cane liquor from her bandana head-wrap. Poured a circle of spirit 'roun the rolling calf, trapping it inside a ring of rum. Adlyn laughed, filled her mouth with the last drop of rum and blew it on her cigar. Fire roared out setting the darkness ablaze. Whack! Whack! The whip stung into the flesh of the beast. The rolling calf pawed the ground hoisted its tail and charged for Adlyn, but she was slippery, dancing and cracking her whip.

'Ha-ha Bull, I know you're in there somewhere. Listen and listen good. The ancestors angry at you in whatever life you in or whatever form you take. Tonight, Beryl and Job will fight back, tonight little Rose grow thorns. If you a bull buck, then me a duppy conqueror!'

So now, here's yo answer. While all a dat was going on, fire galloped through the whole pimento walk. Not one tree survived. So yo see, dat is why all we have left now is jes the name Pimento Walk.

How yo mean that coulda say from start?

Look massa if mi did cut history short yo woulda know 'bout Ocho Rios?

What about maroons in Scott's Hall?

A fi mi fault, a shoulda left yo to loggerhead Buru.

Tangerine

Click. Clack.Eight-inch stilettos strut through the sepia-blushed Parisian morning, soft stabs cushioning a feminine gait.

They were gentle taps, the like of ornate door knockers, beckoning Quartier Pigalle to open her eyes to the soft yellows of morn. She walked tall. A girl needs heels to get ahead. Where did I hear that? She brought the sun every which way her hips sashay. Well, almost everywhere. A pavement princess lurked in the shadows, night-old, postbox still, and cold.

In the distance, a throng of love-and-lust-obsessed youths poured into Pigalle in search of the sex shops. She continued in cold, calculated steps, undeterred. Honey-dipped sun dancing down her platinum-blonde hair; all black trench coat and a velvet choker, nothing underneath—Olympia unhinged from the Musée d'Orsay. They met at the intersection like lava and ocean. Hotblooded boys are terrible at hiding their enthusiasm; the temperature rose but fizzled when met with her icy disposition.

The walk signal came in with a gush of wind and her supple skin peeked through. Still ocean and lava—volcanic glass. Shattered, they dispersed in all directions. Not all males can endure being ignored. A few choice words thrown behind her were proof of this. She was a moving target and didn't care much for boys. Do men really think seeing a woman without clothes is the same as seeing her naked? What are her dreams? What are her fears? Good-time girls were skulking in the shadows down the street from where she came. Easy girls who were scarred by the high price of low living. She was different. Cash was not exchanged between her and clients like at a turnpike. She had offshore accounts, paid taxes, and managed an elite clientele. Powerful men. Fiends for erotic humiliation. But sex-crazed youths who were doped up on whore-chic fashion and internet porn: probably couldn't discern being face-to-face with the pith and core of that life. Pith? I have a sudden urge for orange.

Soon, a tangerine sun sat directly above. It was a perfect day for a munch. Mistresses and dommes had their dungeon downtimes, leaving behind their masks and mirrors, cages, and capes. They gathered at vanilla spots, not only for play but sometimes to scout new members for the club. She ducked into a quaint pâtisserie, bringing the pedestrian and traffic sounds behind her.

The cacophony of sounds jarred in stark contrast inside, where there was a more convivial atmosphere. She sat alone by the window and was quickly served. She tapped her nails around an exquisite tulip-shaped stemware; sipped on her mimosa and took subtle drags on a slim, citrus-flavoured cigarette. The sun came in and lit up her angelic face. Her eyes sparkled and he noticed her from all the way across the room. He started across towards her. The sun melted into the pavement. He was distracted. She disappeared from his sight. Only a few threads of smoke left swirling from an ashtray.

Beguiled and bewildered, he doubled back for his seat, now occupied by her.

Not counting Matthew, the wandering newbie; seated at the table were Olga, a Russian mistress, and Grace (known in these circles as Caribbean Ginger). She was a sultry, promiscuous pied piper who pulled all the sexy young singles to these parties; hoping to swaddle them in latex and whisk them off to the lair.

Olga and Grace spent the last couple of minutes waiting for Tangerine's arrival. Well, mostly Olga who made do with veiled attempts at socializing. Grace, on the other hand, being brash, bright, and imbued with feminine lure, cast a spell wherever she glanced.

Tangerine's cologne announced her appearance. She came in like a breath sucked into the lungs. She wore an unmistakable blend of jasmine, mandarin orange, sandalwood, mimosa, and vanilla.

'Fashionably late eh T?' Olga quipped while rubbing her eyes. Puffy eyes, arrested in red rings and half-closed. 'Yet they're all here,' she continued. 'The flies certainly gather on you, don't they?'

Olga was chalky-white, her hair was done up in a survival bun and a few cascading tendrils at the front flowed straight into her tired eyes. She twitched in her seat in response to every manifestation of light.

'Aren't you going to say something?' Olga deflected attention from herself. Fearful. She shrank from the thought of having turned up to one of Tangerine's parties looking like stale bread.

'You're doing it wrong Olga. It's not pearl diving, you need to come up for air more often.' Tangerine addressed Olga's appearance and not her questions.

Grace glared at them both as if to say let's not do this right now.

'I'm starting to grow dungeon mould; too much time in the den,' Olga conceded with a sigh and unconsciously rubbed her hands.

'Darling, dungeon flowers need sunshine to keep them from falling into total darkness.'

'Yah, but it is the darkness that keeps the clients happy.' Olga mocked Matthew with a cheeky pout.

'You don't have to be pert missy,' Matthew protested.

Grace rolled her eyes at the suggestion that Matthew was a sadist. She tried fixing Olga's hair. Olga fussed but gave in and was hauled off to the bathroom for a makeover.

A girl must fix the cracks in her mask, or she'll not protect her real face.

'Matthew, darling, I know this is all new for you but violating established etiquette is tantamount to moral turpitude.'

'I'm Sorry T, maybe I expected something different.'

'What, a leather-clad bootlicker suspended from the ceiling by a ring in her labia?'

Matthew knew his newbie jitters could land him into trouble or even worse get him banned from future munches.

Newcomers didn't always see the big picture. What appeared to be a pitiful pastry party was a celebration of sexual freedom teeming with symbolism. The tables were arranged in a pentagram, honouring the perfection of the body and the bridge that joined everyone who enjoyed unconventional forms of sexual expression; this was where the magic happened. The erubescent blushes, clustered bodies melting from and into tickled feet and fingertips, all ignored.

That was what they taught at these parties. The secret to munches, or rather the recipe, is to enjoy the whipping, whisking, beating, and baking but always display the result in the window to the public, as a decadent treat. Yes. They all emerged from the coat closet clad in socially acceptable garb. Briefly disconnected from the lifestyle. Such a remarkable volte-face.

'But wait, Gabriel a you dat? What yo doing in di closet maasa?'

I couldn't tell her Aunty D had put me there. I'd have to explain why she had on only a black garbage bag. And why the mongrel dog was in the room in the first place let alone wearing makeup. I backed right out and barred the door to the room with about four different shirts in my hands. 'I was looking for something to wear to church, Mama. Is that the peas smelling like it's burning?'

'Jeezam! A jus pour a cheese pan a water in it, smaddy mus push up di fire.'

Yes man, that fixed her. She spun around and went to tend to the Sunday dinner. But not before stretching her neck, trying to get a glimpse of Aunty D. Not before instructing me to wear the white shirt to communion.

I had no intention of going to church. I couldn't. Someone always had to be at the house to ensure that Aunty D didn't break out and go on the run. She wasn't a Jamaican, but she was living there longer than I was alive. Aunty D was probably more Jamaican than most Jamaicans, but you could spot the difference in her. It wasn't just her brown, straight hair with streaks of greyish-white or her sunless skin that gave her away. No, many whites were also born and raised on the island. It was probably her choice of music and the Euro-chic way she dressed. She taught me that—Euro-chic. Or better yet, the nasal pronunciation of all her Rs. I was born into her hands, and she had always been like a second mother to me even though my mama was her live-in helper. She watched me grow into a young man and I watched her age.

Other than Margot, we were Aunty D's only family. Over the years, Margot kept her bank account fat and her cupboards filled with treats. Like us, Margot wasn't a blood relative. How we understood it was that she was someone Aunty D took care of, and she kept in touch. Now that Aunty D wasn't doing well, she wanted more updates than usual, and she sent money regularly for her care.

Ever since Margot called and promised to send extra money for Aunty D, everybody wanted to take control of her affairs. You think I'm joking? You should have heard mama trying to chat up Margot and how she grumbled when she was asked to give the phone to me. Mama cooked the meals and gave Aunty D her baths, but her mouth always put her in hot water. She said things like, 'Eh-eh, what a way your breast dem 'tiff fi big ooman!' Then got upset when Aunty D put her in her place with a hot reply like:

'We can't all have them slapping like slippers.'

If you had taken a knife to mama's skin, you would not have found a drop of blood. She got a taste of Aunty D's spicy tongue and out of spite, decided never to give her another bath. Well, that was until she heard 'bout the money. She just couldn't keep away. Besides, no amount of insults could compare to the black eyes and split lips I got on the daily. Aunty D's mood switched faster than the hands of a three-card man. She could be anybody. Tangerine I can deal with. She's this classy woman like those in the Sunday Matinees. But when Joan of Arc showed up inna Aunty D, it was a battle to stay alive and protect the poor dogs. Mama said Aunty D was pretending. And if anything, carried on nothing like any lady in the films but more like 'Smaddy weh use to sell har front.' But as usual, Aunty D had the wickedest comebacks for her rudeness.

'Don't be salty. Is it because you couldn't even pay a camel to scatter sand in your direction?' she said, giving mama heartburn.

They didn't like each other at all. I couldn't understand how their relationship soured overnight but Aunty D and I were best of friends. She wasn't always like that. Lucid sometimes and mixed-up other times. On good days, Aunty D and I spoke for hours. We'd chat about literature, music, travelling, and just about anything. She always wanted to go back to Marrakech and take a hot air balloon ride. She went on and on about the lovely weather in Tangier where the tangerine fruit originated. This was when little windows into her past opened and I could peek inside. It was a joke for her to ask me to bury her under the tangerine tree. It had something to do with Greek mythology and her name, Daphné, and being buried under a Laurel tree but her tree of choice was the tangerine tree outside her window. She once told me that she wasn't always such a goddess and had to work on herself. An encouragement she gave to me as well. She also shared some of her bad times with me.

'Gabriel, a woman threw rocks at me when I first came to Jamaica,' she said.

'Yo got hurt?' I remembered asking her.

'Non, Gabriel, just my pride got bruised.'

I loved how she said my name, 'Gah-Brii-El' and not 'Gay-Brel' the way mama and others said it. Some nights we would go out for fresh air and look at the stars. We would run across the common and disturb the peenie wallies settled in the grass. For me, it was always something magical to behold but it seemed extra special for Aunty D. She would survey the dewy pasture with wide-eyed stares as if looking at a glittering nightscape. I would just watch her soak it all in. I had many ideas about what she would be thinking but often concluded that no greater power existed than whatever compelled her to leave the life she had behind. She must have had the worst luck or had fallen into the biggest problem.

I had my own problems too. I wanted to leave home and see the world. After finishing high school, I felt an even stronger urge to get away. Maybe it was because mama kept kneading me to come out of the house and find work. She was sure that Aunty D was going to leave that house to her someday. One time she even tried getting my uncles to put me out. But it would have made business bad for them since all communications with Margot came through me. As much as they wanted to behave rough, they had to go easy with me. That didn't stop them from crucifying me among themselves though. I overheard them plotting to shame me into leaving the community.

'Yo ever si any 19-year-old man speaky-spokey soh?' Uncle P whispered.

'An' soh fulla himself. Bwai fingernail dem look laka fi ooman,' mama chimed in.

'Yo tink him gaan di ada way?' Uncle Glen asked the two of them.

'Wah yaa ask mi?' Mama complained.

'Di man a ask if yo bwai a homo-fomo!' Uncle P whispered.

'People find that out him kyaan stay inna di community,' said Uncle Glen.

'Mi noh tink notn go laka dat,' said mama, trying to diffuse the fire she herself had started.

'Yo eva si him wid a ooman?'

Mama walked out because she knew, whether it was true or not, what they were saying was dangerous. While most of their conversation was funny, it was no joke that it took nothing for a young single man's sexuality to be questioned. Ignorance mixed with the lack of family support was always a deadly combination in rural areas. I wasn't going to allow those three matchmakers to force my hand to prove anything to them though. Anyway, I started dropping hints about an interest in Margot, not to appease them but to be on the safe side.

Margot wanted to fly Aunty D back home. She said something about putting her in a memory care facility now that her health was rapidly deteriorating. We didn't fully understand Aunty D's illness or why she wouldn't jump at the opportunity for better care.

'Non, Gabriel don't let them take me away! Hide me! Hide me in the closet or somewhere!' Aunty D cried.

It broke my heart. I had to convince Margot that Aunty D had no intention of leaving Jamaica. It was news that didn't sit well with Margot. She didn't believe Aunty D was able to decide for herself at that point. I was offended but she explained that she thinks Aunty D's mind was rapidly slipping away. Whatever needed to be done had to be done sooner than later.

Two weeks had passed when Margot called back and spoke to Aunty D. I was trying to leave the room, but she told me to stay close in case she needed me. I heard her speak so clearly to Margot. The best she had ever been in years.

'Margot, ma chérie it's your Daphné. Don't be sad, love. It looks like the final curtain call for me. You've been a sweet child to me all these years but I have one more request of you. I've managed to complete a letter I've been writing for months and had it mailed. Please follow the instructions therein. You will understand why things must end like this.'

A month later, at the close of a sunless day in the country when the sky drained misty white onto the hillsides like a cow had kicked over a bucket of milk in the heavens, Daphné LaCroix took her last breath.

When I turned twenty-one, I boarded a plane to Morocco with nothing but a checklist that read:

  – *hot air balloon ride in Marrakech*
  – *buy tangerines in Tangier*
  – *stare at a glittering nightscape*
  – *go see a play*
  – *for heaven's sake, read the Classics!*

I entered the red maze under a spiced-coloured Maghrebi sunset and the muezzin's call for the fifth salat. His voice echoed from the minaret as that of a mother ensuring that her child made it home before dark.

Click. Clack. My curious feet hurried through the cobbled streets of Medina. Streets that were given over to spice merchants and stray cats. A stiff wind brought an inviting smell of sweet almonds from a nearby bathhouse. But I wanted to be out on the Sahara. Out where the sun was a twenty santimat coin about to fall in dunes of saffron. Out where the night was already pacing on the back of a fleeing dromedary and in just one blink you could miss twilight. I wanted a baptism in that red, hot ocean with the Milky Way as my only witness. And I was hoping that my secrets would be carried away on a wild sandstorm until they were mixed with other strangers' secrets and couldn't be told apart.

I was afraid that like bandulu argan oil, someone would notice that I separated with the cold or that my saffron water was red and not gold. I sat alone in the emptiness and the sand began shifting beneath me. My world was crumbling, and for a moment, I forgot who I was. Then piercing through the deafening silence, her voice came to me:

'Non, ma chérie! You're Gabrielle LaCroix... My Gabrielle.'

Ol' Hige

Junior hurried through the footpath; holding a bankra on his head, covered in ribbons of darkness and a night filled with creatures only God knows. A few moments earlier he was sat in the old kitchen, chin in hand. He gazed across the hillsides into Bennett Hill and watched the moon, with its curved tail laka banana knife making notches in the bucolic sky every time it climbed.

The trail, lined with old woman razor grass, made the climb nothing but self-flagellation to Junior. The cuts and burns were as hurtful as losing to his cousins at straw-drawing. That short straw landed him in the pickle of taking dinner for Miss Kate in Bennett Hill. 'The work of Ol' Hige!' His mother's little horror story of a baby-killing demon which transforms into a white owl came rushing back into his mind. It made him think about Elsie's young baby that had died, making it three such deaths this month alone. And how everyone was now looking at Bev who was about to deliver her first child. Well, not really her first but the first to have made it this far.

He could feel the shadows growing roundabout him and the thought of making this trek twice made him furious. If only his mother had hurried her hand with the meal, he could have gone and come back already. No. She had to tell that ridiculous story flapping about the kitchen like a lame fowl. But as angry as he was, Junior still remembered the shrieks of fright and looks of fear on his cousins' faces as his mother performed her little melodrama and it made him smile a little. She told them how Ol' Hige was an old woman who fed on newborn babies to regain a youthful look and live longer. Junior didn't believe any of it and to prove it, he wasn't afraid to take Ms. Kate's dinner to her.

Before he reached the old house, the grass blades stretched across the path and held onto each other. The moonlight disappeared. Junior called out, 'Ms. Kate!' The dog started barking. And with one hand holding the bankra on his head and the other creating a pathway, he followed the sound of the dog until he was in a clearing and the moon had returned. A little lamplight streamed through the window of the house. It was no brighter than the winkies flying around. The dog saw him. Sniffed the air, wagged its tail, and lowered its head again. Junior hopped onto the four loosed blocks at the front of the verandah and called for Ms. Kate again. No answer.

He touched the front door and it creaked open. He made his way in. A little breeze rushed past him. Something cloud-like shifted above the furniture. At the back of the living room, a shiny nightgown floated in the air with no feet showing. Junior flung the bankra across the room and dashed back onto the verandah. The dog jumped up, tripped him up, and landed them both into a pile of dried flowers and peas trash lying on the floor. A string of baby skulls fell from the top of the baluster and went cackling over the concrete floor until they stopped at Junior's feet. 'Jeezas!' Junior cried out. Him and the dog started rolling 'round in the peas' trash trying to escape but only managing to slide from one side of the porch to the other.

Then a ball of fire came floating through the house and onto the verandah. It inched closer and closer towards Junior. He buried his face into the neck of the dog. The fire stood still.

'Come Brownie,' a woman's voice uttered.

'Ms. Kate?'

'Who else would it be?'

'Bbbbbut the baby skulls…'

'Baby wah?' Ms. Kate asked.

Junior pointed across the porch. Ms. Kate moved the bottle torch in the direction he pointed.

'Pupa Jeezas, look at mi snapdragons,' she cried.

'Iz not skull them deh?' Junior asked.

'Iz mi precious seed pods mi have drying fi plant soon. Yo gwine fine back every single last one of dem.'

'Shine di light and mek mi look fi dem.'

'But wah yo doing out ya anyway?'

'Mama send dinner…'

Junior remembered the bankra. He rushed inside the house to find it. It had landed flat on its bottom, and nothing had spilt.

'Yo neva strike mi as a coward,' said Ms. Kate.

'A mama and har stories dem made mi a little fraid,' Junior replied.

But having witnessed the skulls, the floating fabric and the ball of fire, anyone would think it was Ol' Hige.

'Wah Ol' Hige stories nuh tru?'

'Dem same one.'

Ms. Kate lit the big kerosene oil lamp in the hall and gave

the shade to Junior with a sheet of newspaper and he began cleaning it.

'But something was floating 'round earlier.'

'Floating? But all the same though yo eyes a play tricks on yo. Iz only likl me over di door jamb battling a rat that iz trying to take over the old house.'

'But mi neva si any foot,' Junior mumbled.

'Well from over dat side, you wouldn't see di stool behind the settee. But in any case, yo need vervain tea fi dat weak heart of yours.'

Junior put the shade on the lamp and turned it up until the room was bright as day. He set the bankra on the dinner table and removed the enamel plates. He went and got Ms. Kate's crockery plates and shared the meal.

Ms. Kate motioned to Junior before he could pack the bankra. 'Don't put dem back in di basket just yet. I will wash dem for you.'

'Set dem down ova on di…'

'No ma'am, mi wi wash dem when mi go down. Iz best if mi leave now before it get darker,' Junior protested.

'At least sit down 'til the rain blow off,' Ms. Kate instructed.

'No rain no outta duo ma'am.'

'Dat trail of ants say otherwise.'

A line of migrating ants marched down the wall under the window and disappeared under the dinner table. A few moments later, the zinc roof started crackling laka dry peas on hot stone.

Shi might not be Ol' Hige but shi must be a witch fi know seh it would rain, Junior trembled.

He sat and kept Ms. Kate's company while it rained

outside. She didn't touch the meal. She only asked about every-one down at the house:

'How yo pa doing?'

'Him okay. He was here last week at Dinah baby funeral.'

'Deh try capture the baby spirit nuh true?'

'A uniform him carry for me.'

'Long pants?'

'Nobody no wear short pants to school, ma'am.'

'Well, di first long pants yo pa wear, yo grandpa cut out di back pockets and cut dem short.'

'Him wear dem go school?'

'School? Yo pa was 'bout twenty-five when dat happen.'

'Junior laughed until he almost fell out of the settee.

'Iz nice to see dat him don't treat yo same way.'

Ms. Kate looked over at the enamel plate and noticed that the ants had invaded them and weren't moving. She said nothing to Junior about the plates but enquired after his mother:

'And yo mother?'

'Shi okay to. Just busy ever since Ms. Bev pregnant,' Junior replied.

'Shi and Bev a friend?' Ms. Kate asked in a shocked manner.

'Best of friends!'

'Hmmm. Dat strange to mi,' Ms. Kate moaned and placed her hand on her jaw.

'Not'n noh strange 'bout it. Even when Junie, Ms. Bev sister-in-law talk 'bout how shi pregnant too often, a mama put har inna har place. She say "Ms. College, losing baby and nyaming dem a two different sin-ting",' said Junior, still trying to defend his mother's honour.

'Alright, a hear yo,' Ms. Kate responded to soften the moment.

She got up and inspected the plates closer and realized that the ants were dead.

'Yo not eating the food before it col' and spoil?' Junior asked.

'Let the food sit a little longer. I can even warm it for breakfast. Who knows?' Ms. Kate deflected the attention from the food and wandered off over to the window.

'Shi even carrying dinner for her t'night,' Junior continued.

Ms. Kate shook her head and sighed. *Oh, so dat iz it. Yo brute yo! Yo mean to tell mi seh after all diiz years yo finally getting rid a Bev? From school dayz yo inna di gyal kin cauz yo don't like har. Fus yo ma mek yo dip gourd stick inna grave tek it lick har, shi could'n walk fi days. Then everybody know seh Bev drop, drop from shi likl. Same way madman nearly chop har up a river wid yo same one. Though the other chil'ren seh Bev fall down, only Jeezas can tell me seh a never you push har down. My God, the first pregnancy Bev lose was on account of yo throwing goat head over di fence frightening har. Mi talk 'bout it and mi fool-fool son mek shi put me out and now nobody is there watching dis wicked gyal. Dat ol' demon. A not even can tell Junior to hurry back before Bev eat di food cauz kill him dead him ma a Jezas mumma. But yo too greedy Esmie, yo had to try get rid a mi to. Either way, yo bound fi go a wok house dis time.*

The rain stopped. A loud wailing came over the hill. Ms. Kate looked at Junior, *too late,* she thought.

'Something wrong down the hill. Hurry down and si,' she said.

'Yes, ma'am!'

Junior grabbed the bottle torch. Lit it and flew out into the night. Brownie followed. Good thing the grass was wet or else he would have set the hillside on fire from the number of times he fell in the grass piece. He entered the asphalt road wet and covered in grass seed. A crowd had gathered at his gate. Dogs barked and people wailed. He was just in time to see his mother cuffed in the back of the police lorry and driving away. He ran for almost a mile behind the jeep calling for her until the brake lights were the same size as the bugs' behind winking in the night. Then it was just him and Brownie in the pitch blackness footing it to the police station.

The Jeep went as far as Johnny Gully Corner and no further. The vehicle careened off the road and dropped into the gully. A crowd quickly formed, and men roped their waists and climbed down to see if they could save the passengers, only to find one officer still breathing.

'Lawd di little baby deh right inna di corner… mi swerve! Anybody woulda swerve… mi corporal alright. Him jump. I think him jump. And di prisoner fly through the front glass… where is mi corporal?' said the injured officer between sharp gasps for air.

The men started putting two and two together, piecing the officer's words into a sensible argument before he drew his last breath. Not everybody was convinced a child was sitting in any corner.

'Rum mek yo see things,' one man grumbled.

To give the fallen officer the benefit of the doubt, they searched the ditch for the missing corporal and prisoner.

When they found the other two, nothing could be done for them. The lawman was headless, and Esmie was crushed so badly it looked as if she had broken every bone in her body.

They went to take her up. But to their surprise, it was only a flab of skin in the frock left on the blood-soaked ground.

She was flayed. It was as if a skilled butcher left it there and took the policeman's head.

'Touch nothing down there, a devil bizniz dis,' a woman called out, grabbed her children by the hands and walked away.

People started speaking in unknown tongues and carrying on like they were in the spirit. Some cussed at the top of their voices and a few women cried when they heard that no one survived. Junior and Brownie came upon the crowd and almost ran through it and continued to Gayle, but someone recognized him and stopped him.

'No Esmie bwai dat?'

'Don't let the child si any a dat,' another person instructed.

Junior kept trying to go down the gully, but the adults held him back. At some point he ran out of fight, sat on the cold asphalt, and bawled for his mother. Then the stories started circulating among the people about how Esmie killed babies and Junior's father was an obeah man. Junior acted as if he didn't hear what they said about his family, but they were no longer feeling sorry for him. The unknown tongues stopped. The men pulled up their ropes and left the accident site for the authorities to handle.

'Suppose people fi treat him like how dem seh him ma treat other people pickney?'

A woman tried to move closer to look at Junior's face. The hair stood up in Brownie's back and he began to growl and show his teeth. The woman picked up a piece of bram-bram as if she wanted to hit the dog. Brownie got up on the hind legs and was about to jump in the woman's face when a loud voice pierced through the crowd of people for the dog to behave.

'Brownie! Stop it, Brownie!' said the man's voice.

An ordinary-looking man parted the crowd and came for the boy and the dog. People shuffled about and looked away as if they were afraid of him.

'Get up and dry yo tears Junior!' he spoke again. It was strange how such a twig of a man had a thunderous voice bubbling in his gut.

'Junior!'

'Yes, papa,' Junior answered and with Brownie close behind, they ran towards the man. He hugged the boy and spoke for everyone to hear saying, 'Mark my word, when you all see young Junior again, yo either trying not to meet your maker or him sending you to meet him earlier.'

They then walked over to a dark corner of the road where a swarm of peenie wallies kept flying around laka sparks from pimento wood. The orange embers blazed bright one moment, then cooled black as wood coal. Three of them in the lot had a blood-red light. Junior's father handed him a big quart rum bakl. 'Go and ketch the three red peenies.'

Junior hesitated.

'Do it now bwai or yo prefer going to the deadhouse to get yo mother's spirit? Then yo won't be dealing with this pretty light. Maybe yo get a swarm of flies, smoke, lizards, or frogs. You choose.'

Junior reached out his hands and cradled the spirits, then slid them into the bottle and corked it. They walked back through the crowd and disappeared into the mountains.

123 Acres of Unsound Minds

The first time Johnny set him eyes on Charm, he knew he would have to leave his babymother.

He was driving a Carolla slowly up Spanish Town Road when he spotted her in the crowd of revellers. It was a Wednesday night, and the sound system had the entire West Kingston shaking laka one cheap bass speaker. The uptown fat cats, dressed in designer from crown to heel, paid the selector to keep their favourite tunes in rotation. The occasional weedman passing through the crowd was the night's fan-bearer with some of the biggest Kaya buds you'd ever seen. He brought wafts of sweet tampee and frowzy grabber everywhere he went. A dozen different dance crews had the town-road dust carrying on laka stage smoke. Soup sellers, teachers, police, and soldiers all were bubbling their waistlines. It was as if everyone in Jamaica was there, but Johnny's eyes went straight to the girl in the nurse uniform.

'Pop a whine pon the Carolla nuh,' Johnny called out to Charm.

'And nasty up har uniform? Go wash yo car bredda,' said Pem-Pem before Charm could answer.

To most people, Pem-Pem was a Clarks-wearing, ice pick-carrying bad gyal from Java in Tivoli Gardens. But she was more than she was letting on.

'My girl a neva you mi a talk to still,' Johnny replied without looking at Pem-Pem.

'Wah?' She leaned in and turned an ear in Johnny's direction.

'Mi seh mi naah chat to you!' he shouted over the music.

This time he made sure to look at her.

'But mi a chat to you though. A wah do certain man?' Pem-Pem said while stepping closer to the car.

'Weh yo do, jealous?'

'Doti Johnny? A weh yo get car?'

'So yaa fi switch it up sometimes pon dem. Who di sistren?'

'Don't even look pon har too hard. A mi good-good friend. Yo know wah, come carry har go work to.'

'If unu can wait till mi drop off Queenie and come back.'

'Yo babymother gaan wid har uptown friend.'

'How yo mean gaan?'

'Bredda mi tek mi own two eyes si di chick hop inna the government issued Pajero!'

'A fool shi tek man fa enuh!'

'Yaa carry wi are not fool?'

'Mek shi come.'

Pem-Pem beckoned to Charm to come to the car, and she sauntered across like she was on a catwalk. Johnny's eyes lit up above a broad smile.

'A mi Hannah Town linkie. Him a go drop yo at work,' said Pem-Pem.

'Come pon di front darling,' Johnny said as he pointed over the top of the car.

Pem-Pem hopped in the backseat.

'Wait yaa wah security guard?' said Johnny.

'Johnny stop gwaan like yaa smaddy and drive di doti car. Yo tink mi woulda mek Charm travel alone wid yo a night?'

'Charm, such a nice name. Where you gotta go?'

'Johnny, talk to Charm one more time ahn si if mi ice pick noh pin yo to dah seat yah,' said Pem-Pem, 'Ahn ton off di roof light informa,' she continued.

All this time Charm was just there laughing.

'Straight up a Bellevue Hospital,' Pem-Pem instructed Johnny.

He went through the crowd, slowing down a couple times to allow girls to jump up on the hood of the car and shake them behind. Then when he was out of the jam session, he blasted his stereo and drove like mad. Johnny zipped across town, backroad after backroad until he was at the gate of the hospital.

'Thank you for flying with Air Johnny.'

'Charm come outa di car before mi stab dis deaf man.'

'Thanks, Johnny,' said Charm in an innocent voice, peeking through the passenger window.

'Anytime babes,' he responded and flashed the broad smile again.

Pem-Pem jumped out the backseat and called out to the security guards to come get the nurse before di car man kidnap her.

'A mawning sistren,' Pem-Pem said and gently pushed Charm from the car door, got in and slammed it. Then the two of them watched as Charm's backside swung past the front of the car. When she went through the gate and looked back, Johnny pumped the car horn twice, did a doughnut and left in a ball of smoke.

The following day Charm met Pem-Pem at the entrance of their tenement yard and she stopped her for them to chat. Pem-Pem was sipping on a fruit punch.

'Wait, no hot beer this morning? Yo finally get bad stomach?'

'Something like that. Call it a likl alcohol break,' Pem-Pem replied through bouts of loud belches.

'You not on no alcohol break,' Charm disapproved and went past.

'Hol' up sistren. I want to say something to yo.'

'Mi ago sleep, mi tired. Mi not even come out di uniform yet,' Charm moaned.

Pem-Pem went straight to the point. 'Sistren, don't mek Johnny smile fool you.'

'What yo mean?'

'Mi si how you laugh at all his jokes.'

'Me?'

'I'm not one fi preach 'bout relationship.'

'Then noh start noh sermon, mi a go a mi bed.'

'Alright, mek mi spell it out since yo can't tek a hint. Him ooman a wicked gyal and mi noh waan not'n do yo plus di man occasionally find himself inna mi bed.'

'Wah?'

'Wah, yo don't tink people can love mango and banana?'

'You and Johnny, di way unu gwaan like puss and dog last night.'

'Surprising, noh true? Not even you wid just a wall between wi know anything 'bout it. Yo can live wid dat? It no bother me, we can all even have a go at it.'

'Hmm. Pem-Pem? Yo don't easy at all. Why they even call yo Pem-Pem?' Charm changed the subject.

'Cho, use to mi stage name when mi did swear seh mi a artiste inna grade four and it stick wid me.'

'Just so-so so?'

'Well, mi did borrow Sista Nancy song one time and instead of what a bam, bam fi some reason mi sing what a…'

'Pem-Pem!' they said in unison and a lot of laughing followed.

'Yo know how Jamaican people stay, if yo have a flaw, mek a mistake or have some tragedy happen to yo, a name will stick pon yo,' Pem-Pem lamented.

'Wi just love name things. Wouldn't be surprised if iz a Jamaican responsible fi capturing the Biblical genealogy.'

'Who preaching now?'

'Cho, yoh know wah mi mean!'

'Mi noh know 'bout dat bo mi can prove fi mi point.'

'Gwaan then noh.'

'Look pon dah brejin deh a walk and tip. Wah yo tink dem call him?'

'Mi noh know, cripple?'

'Close, Tippy!'

'Backside!'

'Di man inna di mesh merino wid di telephone scar?'

'Cutty!'

'Bingo! Wah 'bout di man pon di Ninety?'

'Him a bike rider. Rider? No, no wait, him have one eye! Blinds?'

'Nope, Prippa!'

'Wah?'

'Him have to prips outa him one eye fi si.'

Same time an elderly woman came 'round the corner, footing it like one trying to lose weight. Only, she was so thin, that the neon tights she wore flapped in the wind her feet made.

Pem-Pem signalled to Charm with just the flash of her head, to have a go at naming the woman.

'Sexy?' Charm whispered.

'Eh-eh, Ghetto Bicycle cause everybody ride…'

'A suck di two a unu fi come suck mi out,' the woman spun around and gave it to them.

Charm held her hand over her mouth and giggled.

'How yaa deal wid mi so strong, G?' Pem-Pem teased.

'Mi noh eat from mawning, don't test Mi,' the woman continued.

'A noh me, mi just a seh weh di people dem call yo,' Pem-Pem said trying to calm the lady.

'A nuh dat yo pa call mi a nighttime,' the woman fired back.

Charm fell on the pavement laughing and dirty her uniform.

'Pam mi name! Yo hear? Pam! Noh-noh damn bicycle!'

'Alright, Ms. Pam, gwaan a road hot gyal cause yo slim and trim and neat,' said Pem-Pem teasingly.

'Yo know wah to, unu gi mi hundred dollar,' said Ms. Pam as she quick stride back towards them.

'Mi naah gi yo nuh money fi yo go powder yo nose,' Pem-Pem warned.

Charm reached into her bag. Pem-Pem stopped her hand from coming out.

'Si fifty ya, she took a paper note out of her shorts pocket and handed it to Pam.

'Mi ago get som'n fi eat.'

'Anything yo seh muma,' Pem-Pem brushed her off and sent her away.

'Look like mosquito inna tights pon bike back,' said Charm when Pam was at a distance.

'Now yo have mouth? Pam, Charm seh yo look like…'

Charm jumped up and covered Pem-Pem's mouth.

'Eh? Weh yo seh?' Pam shouted from the other end of the street.

'Not'n, yaa. Gwaan yaa Ms. Pam,' Charm begged.

The two got off the roadside still tickled from the encounter with Pam. Pem-Pem invited Charm into her room. She hesitated. Looked at her own door but an excuse was not forthcoming. At least not fast enough to prevent Pem-Pem from doubling down on the invitation.

'My girl mi naah look yo!'

'Mi seh anything like that?' Charm muttered.

'Yo didn't have to say anything. It plaster over yo face.'

'Was jus' thinking I could change first.'

'Keep on yo clothes man, this won't take long. Besides, mi have a plane fi catch later so just come already,' Pem-Pem said, this time seeming annoyed that she had to be begging Charm to come into her room.

Pem-Pem opened the door and motioned for Charm to lose her shoes on the mat. Charm looked inside, opened her mouth wide and gasped laka swamp frog in a swarm of morning flies. It was like stepping out of the Riverton City dump into a suite at the Half Moon Luxury Resort. Cascading drapes, white marble tiles, and a heart-shaped, pink bed that Pem-Pem brought to life as soon as Charm's eyes found their way to it. The bed was a Coney Park carousel with all the bells and trappings for fun.

Charm didn't find Pem-Pem as one to be indulgent in such

luxury or even owning a pink bed. This all made her more sceptical of Pem-Pem's invitation. Like rising water, questions started filling up in her head. *How she own all this? Why is she showing me her place?* Pem-Pem opened her wardrobe and pulled out a red suitcase. Above her clothes on a shelf, a pink strap-on peeped out. It triggered a flush of questions like a flapper valve and the words came gushing out:

'Mi jus' going to say it and done, a what yo involve inna Pem-Pem?'

'What now, Charm?'

'All a this!' Charm said flapping her hands like a rooster getting ready to crow.

'Don't jump to any conclusions, I have receipts fi ev'rything.'

'Even the pink thing in the closet?'

'Especially fi that!'

'Well, it's not my business anyway.' Charm turned to walk out of the room.

'Charm you never strike me as one to judge.'

'I'm not judging you; I just don't understand what's going on.'

'If yo mus' know, the pink thing is part of what I do. I own a shop inna Arcade Downtown, where me sell shoes and things. I sell people like Queenie's friends, people with money and sometimes these men like a girl with a little extra. That's where the pink thing comes in. Now leave it right there so.'

'I didn't mean to pry of such.'

'Don't worry about it. You're my little Lucky Charm. Before mi no memba or yo start question, question me again, let me tell yo what I called yo here for in the first place.'

Charm went to sit on the edge of the bed and listen.

'Eh-Eh,' Pem-Pem called out and tossed her a towel to sit on. 'Have to keep the love nest clean,' she continued. As soon as Charm's behind touched the towel, the bed started spinning laka gig. Pem-Pem laughed as Charm struggled to find her balance.

'Mi know yo woulda do that,' Charm argued.

'On a serious note, mi taking a trip to London and then New York. I'll be gone for a couple months. Mi won't be here fi look out fi yo so mi giving you a heads-up.'

'That sound serious. Am I to be worried?' Charm asked with a sad puss look on her face.

'Yaa good people, Charm and your kind have no bizniz in a place like this. People go missing ev'ryday so don't travel too late. Careful a Johnny ooman. She might not show it but shi jealous and well-connected with some evil people.'

'Yeah, yeah, mi hear yo,' Charm nodded in agreement.

'Another thing…'

'What's that?'

'I want you to handle mi bizniz till I'm back.'

'Which bizniz?'

'Lucky Charm, focus. Money bizniz mi talking. Mi a di banker inna one big partner so mi arrange fi yo collect the money while mi gone. Also, Johnny and Queenie will hand over to you whatever sales money mek down at the Arcade. Stash it and ensure seh the love nest air out from time to time.'

'That sounds like a paying job,' Charm said jokingly.

'Don't worry, there's a treat in it for yo when mi return.'

* * *

It hadn't been a week since Pem-Pem went up and Johnny and Charm were carrying on laka good, good couple. She had him picking her up and dropping her off at the yard. Charm went as far as to loan Johnny some of Pem-Pem's money. It was as if Pem-Pem's warnings about Johnny were in vain, but some women just feel that they can change a man. She allowed Johnny and him broad smile to cause her to think things were over between him and Queenie. Then little by little, Johnny started showing his true colours. First, he had this grand plan to get a visa and go foreign and start a similar hustle like Pem-Pem. Then that idea changed to opening a wholesale because 'ev'rybody mus' eat food.' The plan was to go up, buy the food cheap and pack it in barrels to send down to Jamaica. The only problem, he wasn't getting his visa from any embassy. Instead, it was coming from a man who knew another man working in the US embassy. For two hundred and fifty thousand Jamaican dollars, Johnny got a US visa with a John Crow where the bald eagle should be. Charm had to get a loan from her credit union to put back that money.

Then when the visa issue blew over, Johnny came back around asking about medication to help people sleep or any injection to calm mad people. This time Charm wasn't going to do anything for him, but she was still taking drives from him. This lasted for another two weeks until Johnny asked about what usually happened to the organs of patients who died at her hospital. Charm asked him not to come around again and she never saw him after that.

Two months turned into six months and there was no word from Pem-Pem. Then out of the blue, one morning Charm returned to find the door to Pem-Pem's room wide open and a swarm of police and soldiers in the yard. She wasn't alarmed. She saw these sorts of things all the time. The security forces only police ghetto people.

'You must be Charmaine?' a woman detective came over to her and asked.

'Must?'

'White uniform, Coca-Cola bottle shape, and a long list of other eyewitness accounts I rather not say.'

'Pam, no true?'

'I won't reveal my sources.'

'Yo don't have to, but I know you or your colleagues are short one hundred dollars now.'

The detective smiled and beckoned to another police-woman to come and talk with Charm as well.

'By any chance, are you from Cascade?'

'Yes! How do you know that?' Charm enquired with her eyes bulging out.

'Charmaine Grant?'

'Yes.'

'It's me, Angie, Angela!'

'Angela Prince?'

'Detective Prince now'

'The last time I saw you was what, '92?'

'That very evening after Dwight chased us at the river, Ma carry mi come town to live with my father and here I am ever since.'

'Angie a police…' Charm mouthed the words in amazement.

'Look at you, big nurse and all!' Angie squeaked in girly excitement.

But the happy reunion was cut short when the first detective started gossiping to one of the soldiers about why they were on location:

'She was about that life man, every piece of furniture is Ashley's,' she remarked with a gleeful grin.

'Mi hear seh a few unmentionables got photographed too,' the soldier asked sneakily like he wanted to see the photos but wasn't asking to see them.

'We have to keep this under wraps. This thing is bigger than Jamaica and we don't know who she really was.'

They kept talking about her in the past tense.

'How yo mean who she was?' Charm blurted.

'Charmaine, you haven't heard?' Angie asked.

'Heard what?'

'This is a murder investigation.'

'Murder!'

Charm fell on her knees and started wailing. Angie held her. It felt a lot like when they were little girls to Charm, naked and cowering in the corner of the shop in Cascade. Then Charm went through the full gamut of emotions. She giggled, bawled, talked to Pem-Pem as if she were there in front of her and almost got in a fight with the officers removing things from the room. Just as the officers picked up one item and set it at the door, she marched it back inside. They had to slide her off the bed, peel her from the TV and pull down a drape with her wrapped tight in it.

Later Angie explained what had happened. She was called up to the US to observe the investigation and act as the liaison between the two law enforcement agencies. Apparently, they were treating it like a drug case. She shared as much information as she could with Charm who was still seated in the dirt with a blank stare on her face. Angie pulled out a newspaper article from her clipboard and handed it to Charm. It read:

> *The police struggled to keep the molasses-thick crowd behind the barricade outside the Marcy House in Bedford Stuyvesant. Just last week a machine gun-toting sociopath rained down bullets on a toddler's birthday party in nearby Flushing. Today, the dead body of a pregnant woman was found hanged upside down from a ceiling fan in a police safe house, festooned in entrails and the umbilical cord of the absent fetus. Detective Hugh Hanson who is leading the investigation describes the crime scene as a warzone. He recalled seeing a paramedic in the bathroom throwing up. His partner of fifteen years, Detective Clive Owens, met him in the hallway and retired on the spot.*

Charm stopped reading and handed back the article. She got up mad and stormed off. Angie chased after her. Charm got in her room and slammed the door. Through the door, Angie let her know that she had a different theory to what everyone else was saying.

'Go away!'

'Okay Charm, I'll leave you, but I think you should finish reading the article.'

She placed one of her cards in the centre of the article, folded it, slipped it under the door, and left.

* * *

In the weeks that followed, Charm watched as Pem-Pem's belongings were placed in the open air and all the mirrors flipped around. She saw them lean her pink bed on a wall and she endured the nightly gathering of the people who loved her, coming to celebrate her life by drinking and playing dominoes. It was surprising that Pem-Pem's dead yard wasn't ignored for the Christmas season festivities. But she was good to the community in her own little way. When it got to the ninth night of rituals, a sound system was placed out in the yard, and they played her favourite songs. Even Johnny and Queenie came. Queenie had on dark glasses and a headscarf. She was in deep mourning too. At midnight a band of singers sang a series of dreadful hymns. It was then that Charm surrendered to the fact that Pem-Pem was truly gone. It was then, that she decided to hear Angie's theory.

They met at the waterfront Downtown, close to police headquarters.

Angie opened the conversation. 'How are things at work?'

'Work? Ahhh, that place is like a hundred and twenty-three acres of unsound minds,' Charm said, accompanied by a big sigh.

'What do you mean?'

'Well, we just had a visit from the Minister of Health, and he was pleasantly surprised by staff members serving meals with a shovel. A shovel I tell you!'

'Really? In this time and age?'

'The public health inspector nearly shut down the institution. We've been cleaning ever since.'

'How are you though? How are you holding up?' Angie asked.

'I'll tell you when I get justice for Pem-Pem. What did you want to say to me?'

'I had many questions about the case but because we're dealing with the big and mighty FBI, my superiors were tuck-tailed and tightlipped. For example, why was Zoey at a safe house?'

'Zoey?' Charm said with a puzzled look on her face.

Angie realized that Charm didn't know Pem-Pem's real name. She handed her a copy of her passport. There she was, Zoey McIntosh. Young and serious in the picture but still a sweetheart.

'It doesn't add up,' Angie continued.

'What does all this mean?' Charm enquired.

'Well, you see, to be in a safe house means you're part of an active investigation or you're being protected by the agency. Here's my theory. I believe they wanted your friend to testify against someone, so they had her on some bogus charges like say drug trafficking. Maybe she was targeted on a flight, and they just bring charges that don't exist.'

'Can they do that?'

'It's not a crime for the agency to lie to a suspect to make their case.'

'All this police talk hurting my head,' Charm moaned.

'Hold on, hear me out first. Why was she left alone at the safe house? There's nothing in their report that officers were on site.'

'It was a setup?'

'Exactly!' Angie shouted.

'But what can we do about it? This is the mighty US according to you.'

'True but I believe the perpetrators are from the island.'

'Huh?'

'Look at this matchbook.'

'Jamaica Inn? Isn't that in Cutlass Bay?'

'Now you're thinking like a detective, Charm. Not only the matchbook but there was no mention of the defensive wounds on Zoey's hands, blood in her mouth that wasn't hers nor the fact that her stomach was removed.'

'I don't get it,' said Charm.

'Focus my junior detective. While the stomach removal may signal drug dealers retrieving their product, I believe your girl was a fighter and somebody got a piece of them bitten off.'

'Okay, so they couldn't leave the stomach in fear that they might find the body part?'

'Yeah, and a young entrepreneur from Tivoli Gardens doesn't fit the status quo. In their world, drug mule is a perfect fit,' Angie said with tears in her eyes.

'This is important for you too no true?'

'Charm, I know all this might seem futile, but something evil took place and we're ready to bury it without even scratching the surface.'

'You think there's more to all this?'

'Here's what I think, a lot of homeless people have gone missing in the last three years. At first, we thought it was some demonic rituals from some sadistic gang operating in the corporate area but then my friend in the agency told me that there was a human organ-harvesting ring operating out of Jamaica. You know with tourism being a big thing and all, that is not something the government want floating around in the news or in the international community. So, these criminals were left to do as they please.'

'You think this is linked to Pem-Pem's death?'

'There's something else I didn't tell you. Zoey is not just your friend. She was one of us.'

'What? And she's been treated like a common criminal?' Charm got up and shouted at the top of her voice.

'Quiet,' Angie whispered.

'This is on you, Angie!'

'It's not like that. I shouldn't be saying any of this to you. She was undercover in a sort of way.'

'In a sort of way? You lot used my friend and dumped her,' said Charm while tears streamed down her face.

'There's a way we can make this right, Charm!'

'How, resurrect Pem-Pem?'

'I have credible information that the people responsible are in Ocho Rios. They're operating out of a few unregulated exotic clubs.'

'How can I help you? I'm just a mental health nurse who is going mental myself.'

'I know a way you could help,' said Angie with a piercing look in her eyes.

'Anything! Anything for Pem-Pem!'

'You sure?'

'Dead serious,' said Charm.

Angie searched her face for a while and then gathered up her papers.

'Eight o'clock tonight. Meet me at Clock Tower Plaza in Halfway Tree. We going to Ocho Rios,' Angie instructed. 'I'll fill you in on the drive down.' she ended the conversation and walked back to her office.

Johnny set him eyes on Charm for the last time on a Grand Market night when it was coming on to Christmas morning. It was at a ramshackle go-go club at the mouth of Fern Gully. The little thatched roof place was on the way up Milford Road on the left-hand side to go back into the Great Pond area. It was a shithouse disguised as a bar in the daytime and then a big, big tail-selling shop at night.

The heavy-duty vehicles working on the new highway lay half-sunken in mud and overlooked the certain-death ditches they made as men, like ruttish toads, skipped from bank to bank. Inside was no different.

A naked ooman in the back of the shack was on a makeshift bed of drinks crates and a half sheet of plywood carrying on. She had her legs kicked high like a dead roach and her hands spreading out her nether region and smearing it everywhere, the way a civet marked its branch.

The place was packed tighter than a tin of sardine and carried the same sea scent. About a hundred men were there to do business and a handful of women trying to catch a sale. And Angie and Charm were waiting backstage to spring their trap.

When the time came to go on stage, Charm's feet refused to move. Angie saw her hesitation, crept up behind her and whispered in her ear.

'Do it for Pem-Pem. It has to be you. They can sniff out a cop from a mile off so me or my girls can't do it. Don't worry, we have yo back. Remember the plan. After you do your dance, I'll come and try pull yo off the stage. You must create a scene like you're a mad person. Then I'll leave, change, and come back. Don't worry about a thing. The squad is waiting nearby. Oh, one more thing, the signal is the song. The Sister Nancy. As it left the speaker, government boots will trample this dump.'

Charm drew a breath and swallowed hard. 'Make way for the lady call Lucky Charm,' the selector called out. Charm filled her lungs with air and floated on stage in a transparent thong set. The warm club lights danced off her caramel-coloured skin. The men went crazy! They whistled and flashed their fingers to make the whipping sound. The hands started reaching for her. That wasn't a part of the plan. Charm started backing up laka crab, but they weren't backing down. Angie rushed onto the stage and started kicking them off. The music stopped. The selector spoke over the microphone again.

'What really a gwaan?'

'A mi sister. She not so right in her head and you have her a dance go-go. A police mi fi call pon you,' Angie responded.

'Call police pon who? Anybody hire yo sister? Anybody can go pon stage and collect dem money.'

'A lock yo waan lock mi up inna the cellar again,' Charm cried as she feigned madness.

The men started protesting. 'Leave the ooman alone!'

Then a big gut man came over and got up in Angie's face.

'Leave before som'n wicked reach yo,' he said, squeezing the words through his teeth.

Angie quickly left and changed her clothes.

'You're in good hands darling,' he whispered to Charm.

She nodded and twitched the same way goats battle their earworms, feigning madness.

'Play di music!' the man shouted.

When Charm saw that they meant to keep her, she knew she was closer to finding Pem-Pem's killers. She asked if they could play *Bam Bam*. She remembered her friend and started bawling while she gyrated her hips for the men to gawk over her body. The fat man went on his phone. He was animated. He worked his stubby thumb the way the elderly pump up the volume on the TV remote. Whoever he was texting was surely overwhelmed by words.

Then flashing blue lights busted through the old shack. The siren drowned out the music and sent everyone scurrying. They didn't get far. Police with high-powered rifles were waiting in every direction. They grabbed and bagged every one of them and loaded them in the prison truck waiting outside.

In the melee, fat man decided to grab Charm. The naked woman in the back of the club jumped up with a knife at his throat.

'Just breathe so I can end you,' she begged him.

'You know who yo messing with?'

'Shut up John Crow! You know who you are messing with?'

Angie threw the naked woman a coat to cover herself.

'Good work corporal,' said Angie with a little salute at the end.

Angie helped Charm put on her clothes and they walked out together.

'What now?' Charm asked.

'Now we put them through the grinder until we get what we want.'

Charm laughed.

'What is it?'

'Where was she hiding her knife?'

'I don't want to know,' Angie said and shared a laugh with Charm.

Outside the cops and a few tourists flocked to a soup vendor. They were all enjoying the soup when one of the Caucasians screamed and tossed her polystyrene cup.

'An infant's hand is in the soup!' she screamed again.

'Iz chicken foot lady,' the vendor called out.

Another tourist saw the chicken foot and was convinced that it bore a mighty resemblance to the hand of a small child. Vomit spewed from her lips in the direction of the pot. The vendor jumped out of the way, stepped on a firestick, and hit the pot off the fire. Hot soup wrapped 'round a policeman's ankle. Him rifle drop and go off. It frightened the driver of the prison truck. He sped off and crashed into a front-end loader parked nearby. The bucket came crashing down into a big puddle of water and drenched Angie and Charm. One of the white ladies was so kind to lend them a towel to clean up. Then all hell broke loose. Angie and Charm started stripping themselves naked and ripping out their hair. Before anyone could get to them Angie drew her service pistol and put two into Charm then swallowed a bullet herself. Charm staggered backwards and caught on the jagged zinc fence that fronted the shack.

A handful of cops surrounded Charm. One set tried to remove the rusty zinc from her flesh and the others pressed on the gunshot wounds. She was almost lifeless. The young corporal that was at the back of the club tried holding Angie's head together. It was in vain. The soupy liquid kept escaping from all angles, the way overmixed mortar would flood shallow furrows and waste. The rest of the police secured the prison truck and directed traffic.

A black SUV darted up Milford Road and scratched tires to stop. The officers leapt into action. They were all jumpy by then. They surrounded the vehicle. The police in the front kept the gun pointed at the car with one hand and used the next hand to spin some fast circles. The car windows rolled down and revealed Johnny and Queenie in the vehicle. He had on the roof light as usual. And Queenie was dressed like one still in mourning. The officers searched the pair. When Queenie removed her scarf, her right ear was missing. Only a mangled piece of flap remained. Charm glimpsed the pair, her eyes opened up and she started grabbing a policeman's ear. Memories circled before her face as someone operating a view master. The flashing lights must have been the light source and the man's ear the lever to crank 'round the images. First Pem-Pem showed up in her jeans shorts and mesh merino.

'Him ooman a wicked gyal and mi noh waan not'n do yo plus di man occasionally find himself inna mi bed.'

'Careful a Johnny ooman.'

Charm blinked. Another image appeared. This time it was Johnny and him broad smile.

'What dem do with the organs when people dead at Bellevue?'

Charm kept blinking and the memories kept coming. It was at that moment she figured things out.

But when the dots were finally connected, it was too late, way too late. Had Charm not been so blinded by Johnny's smile, maybe she would have realized that Pem-Pem was carrying his child. She even missed the Caucasians who handed them the towel laced in angel dust. They were so happy to have justice that the light-headedness felt like harmless euphoria until they were gripped by the throes of full-blown hallucination.

As if it would be that easy to tame a monster.

With the heavy makeup wiped from Charm's face, Johnny was able to recognize her. If he was saddened at the sight of her, nobody could tell. He got back into his vehicle with Queenie, did a doughnut and raced back down the road in a ball of smoke.

Charm died knowing that Pem-Pem's killers got away.

Mount Rosser Monkey

Earle Butcher, tall and lanky laka papaya tree, ruffled ooman feathers wherever he went. For a man who didn't smoke, it was surprising that he had two John Crow beads for eyes: always crimson red and black. His skin was this cool, satin-smooth black donkey-eye bead that had been well soaked in a child's jaw corner. This complexion made his ivory nails glisten the way beached nickel seeds take the sand colour. And his teeth lit up pearly white laka Job tears washed up on the banks of the White River. But the real eye-catching display for that old peacock was the bunch of keys dangling from his pants front. That was the real train rattling for the peahens. It was as loud as Poinciana seed pods dried in the July sun for boy pickney sword fights.

But Earle had the familiar face of a contented man, who knew not the autoclaps he was about to face. Earle's mother, Ms. Joyce, had high hopes of him becoming a big shot but it was all starting to feel like waiting on a guinep tree to bear only to find out it was a man guinep. The house was still unfinished, and Ms. Joyce moaned every day about how she could fall on the exposed steel and die before she could see her grandchildren. The nagging became all-out quarrels when a manager position opened at the hotel where Earle worked, and he didn't show an interest in it. One morning before work Earle and his mother almost had a falling-out.

'A rather kin-out mi front give the monkey in Mount Rosser before you work under another black man.'

'Mi not in no obeah bizniz mama!'

'Yo can say anything. Manager after manager and they keep skipping over you.'

'My day will come.'

'If yo follow these blue-eye people they smile in yo face and stab yo in yo back.'

'Even so, we are God-fearing people…'

'There's a time fi everything, noh so the book say?'

'I don't think it meant a time for obeah.'

'Wah ev'rything mean?'

'Yo know what, it's your body, do as yo please. Just don't do anything on my behalf.'

'Okay, I see. So, when yo did a mad over the pretty Indian girl yo never had a problem tying her in the stew peas, though?'

'That was all you, 'bout yo want grandchildren with pretty hair.'

'A still do!'

'Mama, wah mek yo love bring up these things fi a ooman weh seh shi a Christian.'

'Alright, alright! Don't say I didn't warn yo. If yo want that job, yo will have to go and get fix up like ev'rybody else.'

Earle left the argument right where it happened because he knew nothing was worse than mixing up in obeah.

He got to work with the intention of having a week of peace only to find out that it was being whispered that a handful of them were being considered for the job. He knew

Robert, a Bajan, and Ranjeet a Trinidadian. Together, they chased the American and European girls visiting the island. But he didn't know Jacques, a Haitian man working in housekeeping or any of the women mentioned.

After work, the three of them went for the usual tail-chasing at the bars. Nobody talked about the job. They just carried on as usual but deep down they were already sizing up each other and sharpening their knives. Ranjeet was the first one to return to the dormitory. He came back just as he had left. Alone. Tense. Miserable. Still wanting a woman. He was not as lucky as his wingmen. His oil-slicked hair smeared a gloss across his forehead, which brightened the wrinkled frown he wore on his face as prominent as the broken heart left on his sleeve.

'Ranjeet, back already?' his American supervisor, Andy, called out to him raising a bottle of whiskey in one hand, then chinking two highballs in the other.

'Boss da is you?' said Ranjeet shading his eyes under his hand.

'Wait, no little lady tonight?'

'Eh-eh boss, when ah come, they did gone already.' Ranjeet motioned with his arm.

'Come sit with me. Nothing the firewater can't handle.'

'Ah-eh-able clap bamsee here all night.'

'You can sit with me for a few minutes, we start on the same shift in the morning.'

'Ah can. Ah few chinkee of firewater may help meh.'

They both began drinking and the liquid courage loosened Ranjeet's tongue. He poured out his sorrow to his supervisor about the unlucky decline his love life had taken.

'Ah not vex Robert and Earle got gyul t'night. The t'ing is, they did not back mi up in getting one fi miself.'

'They hang you out to dry?'

'Eeh-hi, like a stranger,' Ranjeet said putting a hand to his jaw.

'Well, how about we sit here for another hour or so, see if we can wash this misfortune in liquor.'

'Boss, one of the British ladies aks Robert why he clothes so crushed and hear he 'bout he "i-run" it heself.'

Haha. 'What did she say to him, Ranjeet?'

'She say blo'y hell mate a cahn understand a blo'y thing you say.'

The two laughed so hard that they were snorting drinks. Ranjeet continued dishing on his lekking partners.

'Then Robert finish every line wid a cho similar to a Trini's Cheups.'

'Yeah, yeah I know the sound, hissing teeth,' said Andy hurrying Ranjeet to finish what happened with Earle.

'Boss, di little white lady kept on asking Earle if he okay? Hear me give out maybe he boot deh squeeze he. Robert give me a bad eye.'

'Ranjeet that wasn't nice at all. You know Earle has issues with his feet.'

'Eeh-hi, a wanted she tell he to take off he boot an see di missin' big toe and corn dem on he foot, see if she would still be there asking "Earle are you okay" … Cheups.'

Just then Earle and Robert came walking in with their ladies on their arms. Ranjeet and Andy kept quiet long enough for them to walk by, all the while stifling the laugh until Ranjeet gave out: 'Ah hope yuh lovin' better than how yuh i-run clothes.'

They both erupted in laughter.

For the rest of the week, the three friends were salty towards each other. Then the weekend rolled 'round with an official bulletin that they had a shortlist of four people for the position. Jacques talked it for everyone to hear that he was heading to Haiti and when he returned the job would be his. Ranjeet got scared and asked to be removed from the list because he was quite fine as a dining room supervisor. Before leaving for home Earle saw Robert being escorted off the property by police. They found ganja in his possession. So, then it was just Earle and Jacques. And Jacques made it clear he was going to use voodoo.

When Ms. Joyce heard about the voodoo, she cackled laka layer fowl.

'Voodoo? Haitians use susumba to work dark magic, but Jamaicans eat it. Who should be afraid of who?' she said.

'Yo know how mi feel 'bout obeah man, mama.'

'Yes, but yo think Robert ganja bust so-so soh?'

'It fishy yes.'

'Earle, get real. Yo must fight fire with fire. A mawning we heading to Mount Rosser.'

Earle finally gave in to his mother's wishes. They chartered an out-of-town taxi and headed out the next morning when it was still pitch black. They drove past a cemetery and came to a place lined with colourful flags. A stout, red ooman met them under a big weeping willow tree. She told them to keep their mouth locked until she announced when they could speak again. The driver stayed back and the two followed behind the ooman as she sprinkled salt along the path to a board house with an enamel bath in the centre of it. She wheeled and turned them and wet them with pepper elder and fever grass dipped in chicken blood. Then they had to sit back-to-back with their heads between their legs. After that, she took them one at a time into a nearby banana walk where women clad in red frocks and blue and white bandanas danced to kumina drums. They were placed in the centre of the dancers, who twirled them some more until the spirit took them over. After they went in myal, the ooman questioned them and returned them to the little room to sit again. They had no idea what they were asked or what they had said.

The ooman told them they were cleansed and could speak now. As she left the room Ms. Joyce started blabbing about how you have obeah and then yo have this man kind of obeah.

'People stone people's house top with ice and when they come out in the mawning, the ice melt and so they believe duppy stoned the house. But when this man send a blow on anybody, him send seven devils straight from the pit of hell,' she whispered to Earle.

'Mi still think the worst thing yo can do is get involve with these people.'

'No Earle, the worse thing is fi owe obeah man. The very clothes will tear off your back until you pay every red cent.'

The ooman returned. 'The man will si you now,' she said.

Ms. Joyce got up first.

'Not you!' she said, pointing to the dirt floor for her to sit back down.

Earle crawled out of the room behind her and entered the main house. When they got to a big hall the ooman stopped and signalled to him to continue alone. He walked past a ram goat tied short at the neck, almost hanging. Then a three-foot black puss sat in a birdcage, one crocodile wearing a police hat and a big, black monkey sitting on a bed. When he saw the monkey, his heart started skipping beat laka scratched record.

'Don't worry a won't let him bed yo,' a man's voice echoed from another room.

'Where mi must come?' Earle called out.

'Release the puss and follow behind it.'

The puss led him to a room with ten red candles burning over a heap of bones and an ordinary-built man sat to one side of the room around a firepit.

'Come, before the blood dry on yo,' he said to Earle.

Earle sat before him, and he gave him a candle to hold with instructions not to drop it or allow the light to go out. Earle tried to explain his job situation but was stopped by the man who got up and wrapped his head in red cloth, tied a tape measure around his waist and came back with an enamel plate filled with small bones.

'What yo get yo'self into young man?'

'Iz just a work promotion…' Earle started saying when the man gave him a backhand 'cross his face to be quiet.

'I'm talking to the spirits that followed you here. You just keep quiet and keep your candle burning.'

Earle winced in pain from both the stinging slap he had gotten and the red candle wax that was cooking his fingers.

'Yo must be happy the big cotton tree growing by the Spanish bridge iz no longer standing. The coal man paid good money for you to get justice for his daughter. Yo iz one lucky fellow. A have a great mind put yo back inna one a dem bakl,' said the obeah man, pointing at a stack of glass bottles around a fireplace.

A thick smoke rose from behind Earle and flew up in the ceiling and started moving 'round above them as if looking for a way to escape the room. It shook the zinc, spread, and then turned into a swarm of dead flies that fell on everything in the room.Earle didn't know if he should speak or not. The man scattered the bones from the enamel plate, and one stood upright.

'Look familiar?' he asked Earle.

Earle slowly shook his head from side to side and tightened his face in anticipation of another slap. None came this time.

'You can speak now,' he said to him.

'No sah, I don't recognize it.'

'Iz so long you lost that big toe?'

Earle's eyes widened.

'Yes, it was under the weight of the cotton tree and yo name on a piece of parchment, driven deep inside the bark with a nine-inch nail. Why yo think yo couldn't go any higher at yo workplace? Yo luckily say a bad blow like that couldn't withstand the storm that blow down the tree and mi fee stop coming to keep yo under foot cause the coal man no longer around putting good money on yo downfall.'

'So, this is your doing?' Earle wanted to rubbish the obeah man's argument, but he dreaded being slapped across the face again.

'It will cost yo big time. Mi talking foreign money. Twice the normal amount. Yo need to first reverse this blow and then we can talk 'bout dat promotion. Don't take the Haitian simple. Iz just that my powers go all the way back to Motherland. With the right money, I won't only help yo, but I will deal with all who stand against yo.'

The obeah man sent him back to the ooman who brought him in.

'She will give yo what iz needed and memba don't cross me. Yo don't want me as an enemy.'

Earle held his head straight and got out of the room at breakneck speed. When the ooman tried to give him the handful of vials and candles, he refused them.

'How much mi must give yo fi si di man?' he asked her.

'For today, there's no charge. Just drop a silver coin in the bath pan yo washed in. For the other things, when yo get the job, yo must give us a tenth of everything plus other gifts like hotel stay and so on,' she responded.

'There won't be no other thing. It was a mistake coming here,' Earle mumbled.

'A nuh suh things work. Yo open an account already and I will collect!'

'A can leave?'

'Yo not fixing up yo'self? Stay deh nuh believe seh obeah real. Yo toe, the dead baby, all of it just so-so happenings nuh true? Well, yo must be one born when your mother gone a market.'

'Look lady, a don't want sun catch me in this place,' said Earle.

'Have it your way! The coal man had all right fi set duppy pon yo.'

'A can leave?' Earle asked again.

The ooman moved out of Earle's way and pointed down the hill as if to say he was free to go. He called out for Ms. Joyce who was in the old hut listening to everything. Then Earle stepped off the mountain and left. Ms. Joyce bid the ooman goodbye and hurried to keep up with Earle's long strides. On the drive back home, they didn't speak but Ms. Joyce kept thinking about what she had heard. She put it all together. The coal man, his daughter, the dead baby, and the big toe could only mean that Earle's ex-lover and her people worked obeah on poor Earle. She blamed herself since she was the one who pushed for their relationship. She knew she had to do something about it, but she couldn't let Earle catch wind of it.

Earle went back to work and Ms. Joyce went back to see the obeah man. Weeks passed and Earle stopped coming home on weekends. He would later learn that Jacques lost everything in a big earthquake in Haiti and wouldn't be returning to work. Earle finally got his promotion. He was a big shot now. Living large. He wasn't thinking of his mother or any obeah man. But Ms. Joyce would still sit on the verandah each Friday evening to look for him.

One evening she saw someone come up the walkway to the house. She went out to meet the person thinking it was her son only to find that it was the red ooman who came calling and there was no foreign money to pay her. But whatever agreement was made with the obeah man was sealed in blood and somebody had to pay. The ooman warned that Ms. Joyce and her son would soon learn that everybody ended up paying in some way or another and left.

Two days after Ms. Joyce got the warning she went to church and on her way home, her dress ripped at the back and exposed her slip. At first, she thought it was just dry rot but then every piece of clothing she owned started getting holes. She cleaned the house and sprinkled baking soda in every corner thinking she had roaches. That didn't stop the clothes from going ratty. Then something even stranger started happening. She would be on her bed reading her Bible and the room door creaked open, closed by itself and a weight could be felt beside her on the bed. This went on for a time until one day di heavyweight came and sat on her chest. She screamed out 'The blood of Jesus!' and whatever it was got off her and didn't return. She realized she was under spiritual attack and prepared herself to battle whatever blow the obeah man sent. But she was never ready for what was about to come.

She was out in the yard throwing salt everywhere when the mongrel dog started howling and ran away. A few of her chickens went to roost at midday and plucked out each other's feathers. Ms. Joyce wrapped her head in a red bandana and turned her close inside out laka one chasing away duppy. She went to bed with her black puss beside her. In the night while she kept watch, she heard a clanging through the house. She and the puss went and turned on the lights in room after room only to hear the clanging elsewhere. When she went into Earle's room and flipped the switch, she saw a Chinese man wearing a cangue around his neck. The wooden plank had symbols scribbled in blood. The man, chained around his wrists and ankles, had dead fish eyes, a snake tongue and the squeal of a hog being butchered. Ms. Joyce grabbed the puss and galloped out of the room. She almost knocked the door off its hinges. She crawled under her bed, hugged the puss and her Bible, and started chanting 'The Lord is my shepherd.' The puss hopped up on the windowsill and scratched like mad at the louvre window to get out of the room. A loose board shifted enough for the puss to squeeze through and escape. Ms. Joyce kept her eyes glued to the room door and didn't catch any sleep. The clanging kept going from room to room like a moth to a lightbulb until the sun was coming up. It found its bearings and left.

That was just a warning. The obeah man wanted her to know that there was nothing at the Chinese shop to protect her and remind her that she was being punished.

Ms. Joyce couldn't go to her church for prayers. She couldn't let anyone know about what she had gotten herself into. Instead, she found a little mother-ooman to help her. She told her to burn scotch bonnet pepper in the house at night and sit on her Bible, then jump over a fire three times before going to bed. The next night after doing all that she was told, she fell asleep without any problems. The pepper burned out before daybreak and Ms. Joyce woke to find a tall ooman in a wedding dress and veil standing over her. Ms. Joyce bawled out and cussed some bad words. The spirit lifted the veil over its head. It had only two red holes where the nose should have been.

'Look wah yuh pepper do to mi nose,' it said, talking up in its skull laka somebody with a head cold.

Ms. Joyce started throwing figurines and anything her hands could find at the ooman. The duppy cackled and joined her in destroying things in the house. Pieces of furniture kept hoisting in the air and crashing on the floor. Ms. Joyce found the ash of some burnt peppers in one corner of the room, gathered it up and tried flinging it at the ooman. She blew it back in Ms. Joyce's face and gave her a rahtid slap. The blow landed her under the window, and she tore down the curtains. The spirit lunged forward again with its bony hands, reaching towards Ms. Joyce's throat. The puss head popped back through the window board. The duppy saw the cat and tried to stop. It started to slip and slide around the room laka pigs running on wet concrete. The puss attacked! Ripping the wedding dress, scratching, and biting.

The duppy ran out of the house bawling with the puss still in its hair.

This visitation of demons carried on night after night for almost a week. A rolling calf, a three-foot horse and even a dead baby with a mouth full of maggots that turn into flies with each cry. News finally reached Earle that his mother wasn't doing well. People thought she was going mad based on all the ruckus they heard coming from the house at night. He made plans to go and see her after work Friday evening, to see for himself. He swore that if she was indeed going out of her mind, he would just put her away in some infirmary because that wasn't going to look good for him and his big job.

Friday evening Ms. Joyce was sitting on her verandah as usual when a light bright laka lightning flashed 'cross the sky and a big screech-owl appeared. She remembered as little pickney how she was told that the white owl was Ol' Hige and if it flew over the house three times uninterrupted somebody would die. She pitched the puss out of her lap and ran to the front of the houses and screamed out:

'Pepa! Pepa!'

The owl flew low towards the fowl roost and disappeared in an ackee tree. Then she heard the screech again. This time at the back of the house. She turned and tried to rush towards the unfinished section of the house but tripped over the puss and twisted her foot. The owl made it twice over the roof in the short space of time it took for her to get up and was coming back for the third time. She heard the screech ripping across the sky laka how they sell pound cloth off the bolts in the market. Ms. Joyce knew what was coming. Trying to escape the death blow, she lifted herself, gathered her strength and dashed for the back door.

'Mama!' Earle called out.

Ms. Joyce, frightened by the call, slid straight out the back door and Ol' Hige flew over and left.

'Mama!' Earle called out again but didn't get any answer.

He picked up the puss and walked through the house, looking at all the damages and started thinking that the rumours of madness were true. He came down the hallway gliding on a fancy limp—a new gait to match the new job or just a new way to mask the effects of the missing toe. He got to the backdoor and called out, 'Mama,' almost like a question. Outside, a strong wind came up the hillside and rattled a few steels. Earle noticed that one steel had blood rusted brighter than the others. He inspected it closer, carrying his eyes slowly downward until they were looking at the foundation below. He dropped the animal, grabbed his chest, and bawled out.

Ms. Joyce's funeral was just as eventful as the last days of her life. The final rites on the hillside were interrupted by a John Crow sent to sit on top of the casket. The spectacle sent everyone running. The pallbearers dropped the coffin and watched it glide off the hillside with the bird pecking at the wood. Earle wasn't at the funeral. From the day he saw his mother dead in the unfinished house, he ran off the hill and never looked back. Some people said they saw him sleeping in bus parks, cemeteries and under bridges. Others said that the man crying out 'Ten dollar!' at passing vehicles travelling between Gayle and Ocho Rios resembled Earle. But they weren't so sure. Earle was no longer the sprucy peacock that ruffled ooman feathers wherever he went. And from that time, whenever the red ooman walked through the community people knew that the obeah man was about to be paid... one way or another.

Acknowledgements

My first debt is to Dr. Maggie Hamand, my editor, whose continual support, and vision have transcended my writing ethics. Your warmth and expertise are unfathomable.

I would like to express my greatest appreciation to Taneisha Newland-Spencer, my wife, first reader and best friend. Nothing passes you, not even the kids. This book wouldn't have happened without you.

Martin Goodman, the publisher at Barbican Press has my gratitude for giving my voice a home among writers who have shaped my craft.

Thanks to the writers who were kind enough to interact with me (mostly over social media) and give some inspirational advice that went beyond writing: Sharma Taylor, Lisa Allen-Agostini, Nikesh Shukla and Dr. Brian Lavery.

Finally, I would like to acknowledge with gratitude, the lecturers at the University of Hull who haven't already appeared above: Dr. Claire Griffiths, Dr. Karina Lickorish Quinn, Dr. Sarah Walton and Dr. Chris Westoby.

www.ingramcontent.com/pod-product-compliance
Ingram Content Group UK Ltd.
Pitfield, Milton Keynes, MK11 3LW, UK
UKHW021004210425
457686UK00004B/108